# THE COUNT'S
PRIZE

# THE COUNT'S PRIZE

### BY
### CHRISTINA HOLLIS

First published in Great Britain 2012
by Mills & Boon, an imprint of Harlequin (UK) Limited.
Large Print edition 2012
Harlequin (UK) Limited, Eton House,
18-24 Paradise Road, Richmond, Surrey TW9 1SR

© Christina Hollis 2012

ISBN: 978 0 263 23656 9

Harlequin (UK) policy is to use papers that are natural,
renewable and recyclable products and made from
wood grown in sustainable forests. The logging and
manufacturing process conform to the legal environmental
regulations of the country of origin.

Printed and bound in Great Britain
by CPI Antony Rowe, Chippenham, Wiltshire

To Martyn,
for all your invaluable help and understanding.

# CHAPTER ONE

JOSIE couldn't help herself. Trying to pretend that this was going to be just another job was impossible. Bouncing forward in her seat, she rapped on the glass partition separating her from the di Sirena family's impeccably dressed chauffeur.

'Stop! Please stop!'

The man immediately stamped on the brakes and whipped around to look at her, his face full of concern. 'Is there something wrong, Dr Street?'

'No, no, sorry, nothing's wrong. I didn't mean to alarm you. It's just that I was told the Castello Sirena is very beautiful, so I want to be sure of getting a good look at it,' Josie confided, sinking back into the sumptuous leather upholstery.

Her chauffeur nodded in agreement. 'That's quite understandable, *signorina*. This castle has been called the most beautiful Italian property still in private hands. But, as you will be staying for a month, surely you will have plenty of opportunities for sightseeing?'

'I don't know—I've got so much to do while I'm here. I might not have that much spare time to just…admire it,' she said, smiling. Her excitement at the prospect of new archaeological discoveries was shadowed slightly by the thought of talking about her work in front of students next term, but that worry could wait. She had lots of lovely research to do before then. 'I'm preparing my first course, and I want to bring some of my undergraduate study trips to this part of Italy.'

One look at the surrounding countryside, glowing gold in the sunshine, and Josie knew that seeing the Castello Sirena just as part of a research project was going to be difficult. The place oozed distraction. However, the ink was barely dry on her PhD and contract of employment at the university, so she didn't want to smudge either by not making the absolute most of this opportunity. It had taken endless persuading and presentations to get any funding at all for this trip and she'd been so lucky that her best friend, Antonia, had invited her to investigate their family estate in such a way—the Castello Sirena was usually closed to researchers. Without that cherry, she didn't think her office would have given her the money to travel, and as it was they'd only funded her for a couple of weeks at most.

As a child, she had driven her mother mad by filling their tiny house with muddy bits of 'buried treasure' found in the garden. Mrs Street had sacrificed a lot over the years to see her daughter through university, so Josie was determined to build herself a professional reputation for always putting her job first—at least, that was what she kept telling herself.

She whipped her camera out of her bag.

'Can you spare a minute while I take some photos?' she asked the driver. 'My mum back home in England is never likely to see a place like this for herself. I want to give her some proof I'm actually going to be staying in a castle!'

She had hardly finished speaking before the driver got out and opened the car door for her.

'Oh, that's so kind of you! I didn't mean to put you to any trouble…'

'It's no trouble, *signorina*, as I told you when I took charge of your bags.'

His words made Josie go hot with horror all over again. The summer day was warm enough already, without an embarrassing reminder of that scene at the airport. She was so used to fending for herself, being greeted there by a stranger in a sharp suit and totally black sunglasses had made her instantly suspicious. She had refused to hand over her things until she'd checked his ID.

'Then thank you.'

Josie stepped out of the car and into the furnace that was Tuscany in July. She took a few quick snaps along the tree-lined drive towards the great castle on the hill, then dived back into the luxury of the di Sirena limousine as soon as she could. Its air-conditioning was a wonderful treat on a day like today.

'What was that lovely smell?' she asked as they set off down a cool green corridor formed by trees planted on either side of the mile-long drive.

'This lime avenue is in flower.' Her driver waved his hand towards the leafy green canopy overhead as they cruised along. 'Insects love them. You can hear them buzzing from a long way away. Count Dario once told me there could easily be several million bees working away on the flowers at any one time.'

Josie thought that was a very fitting image. Count Dario was the brother of her friend Antonia. Josie had never met him but, from the tales Antonia told about him, the man sounded a real drone. He partied every night and loafed around his estates during the day while every-

THE COUNT'S PRIZE

one else did the actual work. It was no wonder he knew all about bees.

'Stroll beneath these trees when the sun is high above the old *campanile*, Dr Street, and you'll hear them purring like a Rolls-Royce engine.'

Josie sighed. 'It sounds lovely.'

'You should make the most of this place while you have it all to yourself,' the driver said. 'It was another late one last night, so everyone is still asleep. We've already been told the current crop of house guests won't be taking lunch today. Signora Costa, the housekeeper, will be making arrangements for you to eat alone, Dr Street.'

Josie shut her eyes in relief and thanked her lucky stars. The *castello* might be a new experience for her, but she had holidayed at Antonia's apartment in Rome and the di Sirena family villa in Rimini several times. In both places, her best friend's neighbours were all seriously grand. They were lovely people, but that didn't stop Josie feeling as out of place as a sardine in a tank full of angel-fish. She always enjoyed playing with little Fabio while his mother, Antonia, went shopping; it was the evenings spent listening to people she didn't know talking about spending three months skiing and visiting places she had only seen in colour supplements that Josie found hard work. Making small talk was her idea of hell. She was taking it for granted that Antonia's older brother would be nocturnal because of his notoriously wild social life. That suited her. It meant she would be free to work in and around the ancient splendour of the Castello Sirena all day and be fast asleep before he surfaced, ready for another night on the tiles. With the limited amount of time available to her, she didn't think she could afford to waste a single day.

At the thought of what Count Dario would be doing in the evenings, it was impossible not to feel a twinge of envy. She looked around at the sun-drenched acres of the Castello Sirena. Although she loved her work, Josie sometimes felt like a hamster on a wheel. She had to keep forging ahead just to pay her bills, while people like Count Dario had everything handed to them on solid silver ancestral platters.

When she'd first started sharing rooms with Antonia at university, she'd wondered if their wildly differing backgrounds would poison their friendship. Instead, it was a source of endless amusement. And when either of them hit rough times, the other was there with support.

Loyalty was important to Josie. She'd thought she had found it in her ex-fiancé, but she had been proved as wrong about him as Antonia had been about her own partner, Rick. When Antonia got pregnant, Rick had abandoned the poor girl instantly. Josie helped her best friend to pick up the pieces, but secretly she thought Antonia was better off without the guy.

After her own experiences, Josie was developing a very jaundiced outlook when it came to men. When her friend decided that she wanted to stay at home with her baby, rather than getting back to her studies, it was a blow to Josie. Her work just wasn't the same without her friend. That was why she was so looking forward to this project. It gave her a great chance to work, with the prospect of catching up with Antonia and little Fabio when they got home from Rimini.

Josie had to admit that a bit of her envied her friend's freedom to choose…

'Right, here we are.'

The chauffeur broke into her thoughts as he pulled up at the great front entrance to the *castello*. Josie got out of the car, pulling her skirt straight. As she looked up at the rambling old building she fiddled with some unruly strands of brown hair that had escaped from her ponytail. Imagine living in a place like this. The high stone walls and towering fairy-tale turrets were so beautiful. She wondered how many warriors had cantered up to this awe-inspiring entrance over the centuries. Its great oak door was studded with huge iron nails and bleached by hundreds of bright summer days like this one. In the centre, the figure of an iron mermaid, copied from the di Sirena family's crest, looked down on her with scorn.

Behind her, the chauffeur drove off to deliver her luggage to the back of the house. Conscious of being the latest in an endless line of visitors over the years, Josie advanced, caught hold of the great iron bell pull on one side of the door and got ready to pin on her best public smile.

Count Dario di Sirena was bored. As usual, he had entertained his guests lavishly the night before, but that meant there was no one up and about to entertain *him* yet. The yachting club members had been busy into the early hours, sampling the wide range of wines in the *castello*'s cellars. Alcohol had no particular attraction for Dario any more, so he was letting his guests sleep it off this morning while he made his usual early start. That was fine for them, but it left him short of a tennis partner. Hitting balls pitched at him by a machine was no substitute for a proper match. Not that many visitors to the castle ever seemed keen on sport, although they never refused his hospitality. His guests' interest in him only as a name to drop was beginning to irritate Dario.

*Just for once I'd like to find someone willing to forget my rank and give me a good hard game,* he thought, scything the heads off a dozen innocent moon daisies with the head of his racket. He opened a green swathe through the sea of calm white flowers. Seeing it, he took another pass, sending florets spinning through the sunshine. As he was idly wondering if it might be satisfying to try scything the whole meadow like that, he heard one of his cars.

Shading his eyes against the relentless sunlight, he watched it stop briefly outside the house while a girl got out. Dario quickly tried to remember who this new visitor could be. Surely it wasn't Antonia's friend? She wasn't supposed to be arriving until the twelfth. He checked the date on his watch, and grimaced. Today *was* the twelfth. He sighed. Since he'd inherited his title, he found time passed so quickly that all the days merged into one another. Time slipped away like water through his hands, and what did he have to show for it? A golf handicap that was fast approaching zero, and enough frequent flyer miles to circumnavigate the solar system.

Anything Dario wanted, he could have.

*Except a good reason for getting up early,* he thought.

Shouldering his racket, he strode over to introduce himself to the new visitor with a smile.

Antonia had told him that her best friend was here to work and was not to be…distracted. The way his sister described Dr Josie Street, Dario half expected to be playing host to an eccentric nun. The woman he now saw trying to raise the alarm outside his house was far more appealing than that.

*Although...* he considered, looking her over with a practised eye, *she's doing her best to hide it.* Josie's tightly drawn-back hair, concentrated frown and shapeless clothes all indi-

cated a woman fighting her natural good looks
as hard as she could. She certainly fitted his
image of an English academic. *Hmm...maybe
someone should tell her that there's more to life
than study,* he thought in passing as he drew
closer to her.

Years spent toiling on archaeological digs as a
student meant Josie was no weakling, but the
bell pull defeated her. She tried knocking on the
door, but its six inches of solid oak deadened all
sound. The chauffeur was bound to have warned
the other staff that she was on her way, but Josie
suspected it would be some time before they
came to check. When one final haul couldn't
dislodge the bell pull she stood back, brushing
flakes of rust from her hands in disgust.

*'Buon giorno.'*

She jumped at the intrusion, and swung
around. A man was walking towards her out
of the sun, and the mere sight of him made her
stand and stare. Towering head and shoulders

over her, he was all toned limbs and easy grace. His unruly black hair and flashing eyes were teamed with a golden tan and immaculate tennis whites. It was a breathtaking combination, and she suspected he knew that only too well. In contrast to Josie's dusty travelling clothes, everything he wore seemed brand new. The state-of-the art tennis racket he bounced against the palm of his left hand as he drew closer didn't look as if it had ever been used in anger. It even had daisies woven into its strings.

*I wonder if they were threaded there by some girl?* Josie thought, glancing around to see if this vision was making his way over to someone glamorous who might be standing nearby. The courtyard was otherwise deserted so, wonder of wonders, he must be heading straight for her.

She didn't need to be told who it was. Those soft brown eyes and dense dark lashes were instantly familiar. This must be her host, Antonia's brother. To Josie's eyes, he looked even more wayward than his reputation.

'Allow me to introduce myself. I am Count Dario di Sirena.'

The vision confirmed her suspicions with a voice like warm honey. In a grand gesture he reached for her hand and swept it up to his lips for a formal kiss.

Josie's immediate reaction was shock. 'Why aren't you in bed?' she blurted out.

Dario raised his eyebrows. 'I assume that isn't an invitation?'

Josie snatched back her hand and retreated, blushing furiously. She had got off on the wrong foot in spectacular style, even for her.

Dario smiled, ignoring her awkwardness. 'You must be Josie.'

'Dr Josephine Street, yes,' she muttered, ignoring the little voice inside her telling her off for sounding so sullen. Meeting new people had never been easy for her, and it was ten times harder when they were this gorgeous.

'That's very formal, Dr Josephine Street!' Dario teased, but Josie was too flustered to smile back at him and flirt like he was no doubt expecting.

'I'm a very formal person.'

'Then allow me to say that it gives me the greatest pleasure to welcome you into my humble home,' he announced with mock gravity. As he spoke, he inclined in a semi-formal bow. When Josie pointedly refused his unspoken invitation to join in the joke he straightened up again, but he was still smiling.

Josie knew that hiding her shyness behind a brave face often worked, so she fell back on that. She lifted her chin and returned his gaze boldly. This was a man who was at ease in every situation—she had learned that much from Antonia's stories. The same stories that had led her to surreptitiously search for him on Google the other night. Neither the gossip columns nor Antonia had exaggerated. His aristocratic bearing made those anecdotes all too believable, and one look at Count Dario di Sirena showed that his charm ran deep. He was as gorgeous as he was imposing, and radiated an inner assurance that all the wealth and power in the world couldn't buy. Dario in the living, breathing flesh was a different prospect altogether from his sister—Josie's cheerful, chubby friend. Without a doubt, he was the best-looking man she had ever seen. The way he looked at her was its own distraction: it set her firmly at the centre of his universe.

It took a supreme act of will on Josie's part to remember that most men had the attention span of fruit flies. She took it for granted that when she failed to massage his ego Dario would soon lose interest and disappear. That tactic had worked only too well for her in the past, even though she hadn't done it deliberately. Men seemed to vanish, whether she wanted them to or not. An experienced charmer like Dario wouldn't waste his time in trying to pursue her.

'I'm surprised you chose to come straight here instead of staying at Rimini with Antonia and little Fabio first, Dr Street,' he said conversationally, trying to penetrate her awkward silence.

The spotlight of his attention paralysed Josie. Somehow he seemed to be blinding her, even though his face was in shadow. She moved uncomfortably, trying to persuade herself it was the sun that was sending her temperature off the scale.

'You can call me Josie,' she mumbled. 'I've stayed at your villa there before, and felt that I rather cramped Antonia's style. She always tried to include me in her entertaining, but all those posh neighbours with their stories about people and places I didn't know were...' She groped for a way to put it politely.

'Not quite your cup of tea?'

Dario's words were slow, but the merriment in his eyes was quicksilver. Hearing his beautiful Italian accent caress such a typically English phrase, Josie felt it melt the veneer of sophistication she had tried to put on. The fierce heat of embarrassment rushed up over her breasts and stained her face with a blush again.

'The chauffeur took my luggage away with

him and left me here on my own. I was trying to work out how to attract someone's attention.'

'You've got my attention now,' Dario said with calm assurance, and something deep inside Josie flared to life, wishing that were true. Impervious to Josie's internal turmoil, Dario reached out to the bell pull and flicked aside a small catch that Josie hadn't noticed. It was keeping the iron rod clamped in place.

'Ah—of course. Thank you.'

She put out her hand automatically, but he caught it before she could connect with the heavy iron ring. For a split second she experienced the grip of his strong brown fingers again, then his touch fell away.

'I wouldn't. That's the *castello*'s original fire alarm, and this is the assembly point. It operates a big bell that gathers everyone within earshot and I don't think either of us would want that, would we?'

Josie shuddered. The idea of being the centre of attention horrified her—unless her audience was as warm and friendly as this man. With a smile that told her he knew exactly what she was thinking, Dario flicked the safety catch back on.

'To ring the bell, you need to get up close and personal with Stella Maris here,' he said, nodding towards the iron mermaid. 'One of my forebears had a wicked sense of humour.'

Dario seemed to have inherited it. Sticking out his index finger, he pressed the mermaid firmly in the tummy button. An astonishingly loud ring drilled into the interior of the house.

'Ah! Was this one of the inventions of the eighth Count? When Toni suggested I came here, I read everything I could find about the *castello*,' Josie gabbled to cover her embarrassment.

Dario looked bemused, then shrugged. 'If you say so. I have no idea, I'm afraid. Whoever thought of it must have wanted to deter honest women.' Dario gave her a wickedly expressive look.

Josie blushed again. Beside Dario, she felt

like a hedge sparrow matched against a peregrine falcon. He was totally at ease in his sunny surroundings, and dressed to enjoy them. Josie wasn't. Her shoes were comfortable but clumpy, while her chain-store skirt suit was totally out of place beyond her university's lecture theatre.

Within seconds, the great main door creaked open and a servant showed them into Dario's home.

The *castello*'s entrance hall was dominated by a huge stone hearth. The fire back was a copy of the di Sirena family crest, with more mermaids like the ones Josie had seen discreetly stamped on Antonia's luggage.

'There go your things,' Dario observed as a member of his staff swept past carrying a suitcase in each hand. 'They'll have put you in the West tower. That means you won't be disturbed by any of the yachting club who stayed here last night. They're all in the East wing. Come on, I'll show you up to your suite.'

While Josie stared in wonder at the entrance

hall's carved ceilings and wooden panelling, he was taking the marble staircase two at a time. When he called to her, she had to run to catch up.

'I'm sure you must have better things to do, Count Dario. Don't let me put you to any trouble.' Her voice echoed through the foyer.

He looked down at her sharply from his vantage point on the first landing. 'You're already a friend of the family, Josie, so to you I'm Antonia's brother. Just call me Dario. It really would be my pleasure to show you to your suite,' he finished firmly.

Josie followed him, although she had her reservations.

'Are you sure you can find it?' she said drily as they walked through a warren of corridors. All the flawless white plaster and polished woodwork made them look alike to her.

'I have been rattling around inside this place all my life. Hasn't Antonia told you why these floors are so shiny?'

Josie shook her head, smiling at the incongruous image of Dario with floor polish in hand.

'I'd tie dusters to her feet and push her up and down, along all these miles of corridors. No matter how upset she was, that could always make her laugh.'

'It's hard to think of anyone being unhappy in a place as beautiful as this,' she murmured.

'People forget—there is more to life than just a lifestyle.' Dario sighed, pushing open the nearest door. They were in the oldest part of the castle, where a huge lookout tower had been built within the shelter of its thick stone walls. It had been completely modernised, with a circular staircase leading up to a self-contained suite arranged on three floors. The first floor was laid out for dining and relaxing, while the second contained a bedroom and en suite bathroom.

'—and finally,' Dario announced as he led her up beyond the second floor doorway, 'there's something I call the solar...'

They had reached the top floor and he stepped

out into a large circular room with windows facing in every direction. There were glass panels set into the roof too, so the whole space was flooded with light. It felt almost as free as being outside, but with the benefit of a sophisticated air-conditioning system.

'Wow…' Josie breathed, but couldn't say anything more. She walked around the sunlit interior, taking in its panoramic views of the Tuscan countryside. The atmosphere outside was as clear as vodka. Pencil-slim cypress stood out like exclamation marks against rolling fields of arid grass, sunflowers and the green corrugations of the estate's vineyards.

'You should see it after nightfall,' Dario told her, waiting until she paused before strolling slowly over to stand beside her. 'It's a scene of black velvet, full of possibilities. Headlights streaking along the Florence road…is it a triumph or a tragedy, a baby arriving or a lover departing? It'll be hard for you to pick out the little farmhouses scattered across my land until you know the area better, but by night Luigi's house, Enrico's olive grove and Federico's farmhouse will all be recognisable.' His voice dropped to a wistful note. 'I come up here sometimes to sit in the silence and wonder what they're all doing.'

He was standing so close to her, Josie could feel his presence as well as catch the delicious drift of his aromatic aftershave. It gave her a tremulous feeling deep inside her body.

*What's happening to me? I've come here to work,* she thought in alarm, glancing up at him.

Dario was gazing out across the view, lost in thought. At that moment, as though feeling her gaze fall on him, he turned his head and their eyes met. Another sensuous ripple thrilled straight through her.

And, as if knowing what was on her mind, Dario granted her a slow, sweet, irresistible smile.

# CHAPTER TWO

JOSIE'S mind and body churned as she almost drowned in Dario's gaze.

*It must have been like this with Andy and that woman at the university,* she thought with a shiver. *I can't risk getting between this man and the girlfriend he's bound to have hidden away somewhere.*

After what felt like an eternity, she managed to regain enough control to step away from him, as if to take a tour around the room.

'This suite is wonderful, Dario, but it's way out of my league. Don't you have anything smaller?' she asked, desperately trying to bring them both back to earth.

He looked startled for a moment, then laughed.

'This isn't a hotel! As I kept telling Antonia, you don't have to pay anything at all for your visit, Josie. As her friend, you have a standing invitation to stay here whenever you like, for as long as you like. Surely she passed on my message?'

'She did, but I always pay my own way.'

'And the local hospital fund was very grateful when I forwarded your contribution.' Dario grinned. 'So why don't we pretend your generosity qualified you for a complimentary upgrade?'

Josie hesitated, but decided that she had made her point.

'In which case, thank you, Dario. But I'm afraid you won't get much chance to look out of these windows while I'm staying here,' she told him, and herself, briskly. 'This looks like the perfect place for me to spread out my finds and paperwork. It's well away from everyone else, so we won't disturb each other. Thank you for bringing me up here.'

Dario gave her a smile of silent amusement. The meaning in her clipped words was only too obvious. She wanted to be alone, so he slowly headed back towards the door.

'You're trying so hard not to let yourself go, aren't you?' he murmured, just loud enough for her to hear.

'I don't know what you mean.'

He turned to face her, and then grinned again. 'That blush tells me you've been taking too much notice of Antonia's stories, Josie.' He chuckled, his rich Florentine accent making her name sound incredibly beautiful. 'Be assured that, as my sister's best friend, you are quite safe. From me, at least.'

'Anyone coming on to me would be making a mistake, Dario,' she said firmly, 'and I'd be making an even bigger mistake if I fell for it,' she added. Her voice stopped his smile in an instant.

'I suppose that's understandable, when you've seen what has happened to Antonia.'

'And to me.'

His eyes flashed dangerously. 'You don't mean that waster Rick tried it on with you, too?'

'No—no! I just assumed Antonia had told you about—' Josie stopped, and mentally hugged her friend. Antonia must have been very discreet. 'That is…I mean…I had a similar experience, though it was nothing compared to what Toni's been through. At the time I tried to warn her, but it was hard when she was so happy.'

His expression turned into one she couldn't quite identify. 'Knowing Antonia, trying to warn her off was a rash move. And yet you're still friends?'

'Of course.'

Dario's dark, finely arched eyebrows shot up. 'Weren't you afraid she would dump you for trying to make her see sense?'

'Oh, yes, but I felt I had no choice. I couldn't bear to stand back and watch her throw away all her hard work for a man who was nothing but a lightweight—if you know what I mean.'

Her glance flicked around the palatial surroundings of her suite. She hoped he wouldn't take her words personally. Seeing all the brand new luxury decorating the age-old splendour of the Castello Sirena, Josie decided she was going to like staying here, despite its attractively distracting Count.

'I most certainly do know. I get plenty of gold diggers prospecting around me,' he said grimly.

Josie laughed. 'The only digging I'm interested in is the historical sort. So if you've got any ancestral skeletons hidden in your wardrobe, I'm the one to find out where their bodies are buried. *Your* dark secrets are your own affair, though!'

She was still glancing idly around the room as she spoke. When he didn't reply, she looked back at him quizzically. For a second, there was such a depth of feeling in his irresistible dark eyes that not even Dario could hide it. The instant she trapped his gaze, the look vanished. His expression was left as bland as any first-time house guest could wish for, but Josie wasn't fooled for a second.

In that instant she had seen a genuine reaction from a man who must be as used to putting on a public face as she was. Somehow, Josie knew, she had touched Dario di Sirena on a raw nerve. The man was hiding something. She had no idea what it was, or what she had done to provoke him.

All she knew was that she would have to be on the alert from that moment on.

Dario rarely allowed himself to be anything *but* alert. He had been born an aristocrat, and now fell back on the full force of his upbringing. He kissed her hand again and covered his momentary lapse with his most charming smile, which usually distracted even the most stubborn woman. Except…it didn't have that effect on Dr Josie Street. Right now her green eyes were as bright and hard as emeralds, and her long silky lashes could do nothing to soften her curious, intelligent gaze. For a moment, she'd forgotten to be shy. Then a lock of hair dared to escape from the band that was holding her severe ponytail in place and she snatched back her hand. The wayward strand was scraped irritably behind her ear and she turned her back on him to fuss with her suitcases.

Dario chose to take the hint. 'Goodbye, Josie. I hope you enjoy your stay here.'

'I'm sure I shall, Dario. Especially when Toni and Fabio get back here next week.'

'You could still join them both in Rimini now, if you like.' Dario lifted his tennis racket again and began idly spinning it over his palm. 'I could arrange transport for you right away.' For some reason, the thought of Josie and her all-too-perceptive gaze staying here for the week made him uneasy.

'No, thank you.' She glanced over her shoulder at him with a glint of green ice. 'As I said before, I'd rather work here than gossip with the beautiful people of Rimini.'

He raised his eyebrows again. 'It's a rare woman who would choose that.'

'Not rare, just honest,' she countered.

Dario tipped his head in salute. 'That quality

is in short supply in the circles I move in. I can see why you would have difficulty fitting in.'

She shrugged. 'Research demands honesty, and it gets to be a habit. That's all.'

'I'll bear that in mind,' Dario said as he left, wondering what it would take to make Dr Josephine Street loosen up.

Josie couldn't wait to plunge out into the estate and start exploring. She unpacked as fast as she could, intending to get busy straight away, but her suite was as distracting as Count Dario di Sirena himself. It seemed odd to hang up her cheap white T-shirts on beautiful hand-made padded hangers filled with lavender. The marble wet room that was part of her en suite bathroom was an irresistible temptation as the sun climbed higher outside. Tearing off her shoes and tights, she padded around in it barefoot for a while.

By the time she had changed and finished exploring the three floors of her hideaway in the tower, Dario's other guests were in a holding pattern down in the courtyard. Watching all those chauffeur-driven limousines and prestige sports cars jockeying for position was an entertainment in itself. Josie spent much more time than she meant to with her elbows on her windowsill, staring down at the magnificent procession.

It was only when the Count himself came into view that she dodged back from the window. She moved as though she had been burned, not wanting Dario to think that her claim to be busy was just empty waffle.

*Work first, play later,* she kept reminding herself, although, for her, *later* never quite seemed to arrive.

Antonia was always joking that no one would ever catch Josie idling. Josie wasn't sure she liked what that said about her, but she really did have a lot of work that had to be done before the new academic year started.

Italy and its history had fascinated Josie since she was a child. Pottering about in her back garden, she was always unearthing things and taking them in to school. One piece had turned out to be a broken Roman brooch, lost by a woman over two thousand years ago. That single piece, and an inspirational teacher, had really fired Josie's imagination. Now, twenty years later, she was here in the land of the Romans preparing to inspire others, allowed to design a whole new course! She was acutely conscious of her luck, and grateful for the sacrifices her mother had made. The downside was the extra pressure she felt to make the best of all her chances.

That was why watching Dario walk across the courtyard was bound to disrupt her plans. Something about him drew her back to the window again like a flower to sunlight. He had swapped his tennis kit for taupe jodhpurs, a white shirt and a pair of highly polished riding boots. The pale clothes showed off his exotic colouring perfectly. Josie could hardly believe her luck. Hard work had brought her here to Italy, and now she was staring down at a drop-dead gorgeous guy from a tower that would have made Rapunzel sick with envy. Dario strolled across the forecourt, heading for the shade of the lime avenue like an emperor inspecting his lands. His leisurely strides were deceptive. They ate up the distance so quickly that soon the canopy of lush green leaves would hide him from view.

Then Count Dario di Sirena stopped, turned and looked quite deliberately straight up at where Josie was watching him from her window. She was transfixed. Something made her raise her right hand to wave, but another impulse snapped it straight back down to her side. She could imagine how her mother would sigh if she knew about this little tableau. Mrs Street would go all misty-eyed and lose herself again in the story of how she had met Josie's father. Josie hated that. Her mother was the sad proof of how easy it was to misjudge a man, and it always dragged her own personal error of judgement out into the light again.

Dario continued to look up at her thoughtfully

for a moment, then nodded a salute and turned to disappear into the trees. In a burst of embarrassment, Josie ducked away from the window and scrabbled around to find her notebooks and camera. This was a working trip, with a lot to do and not much time in which to do it. She had to build her reputation as a serious academic. Gawping at Dario di Sirena wouldn't help *that* at all! Packing her things into a messenger bag, she slung it over her shoulder and headed down to the castle's entrance hall.

Once out in the sunshine again with a map provided by the resident housekeeper, Josie was careful to turn her back on the lime avenue. She set off in an entirely different direction from Dario, in case he got the impression she was following him. Heading out to the far side of the estate, she passed through shady groves of ancient olive trees and fragrant citrus, soaking up the sun. She wanted to reach the point where the di Sirena estate's grand gated drive met the twisting country road that idled past on its way to Florence.

She had spotted two men working on a stone wall there. In her experience, boundary walls were magical things. All through history, people had haggled over them and changed them, climbed over them and dropped things in the process, or hidden special little items in between their stones or under their foundations. She set off towards the workmen in a hurry, but the intense heat soon sapped her energy. Strolling along was the only way to travel on a beautiful day like this. A skylark lifted off from right under her feet, while corn buntings and yellowhammers rattled away from every thicket she passed.

She had drunk almost a whole bottle of water by the time she'd toiled all the way over to the workmen. One of them had already left in search of his dinner. The other was clearing up ready to disappear, too. Luckily he was a fund of stories, with a keen eye for what he called 'little bits of something and nothing'. She was listening to him intently when she felt, rather than heard, a drumming sound reverberating through the parched grassland beneath her feet.

It was Dario. Mounted on a magnificent bay horse, he was cantering towards where she stood.

Josie planned to call out a casual, carefree hello, as though his appearance didn't make her pulse immediately speed up. However, as she watched him ride towards her like a prince, come out of a storybook to claim her for his own, the words somehow caught in her throat and she was silent as he drew up in front of her.

He grinned. 'I've had friendlier greetings!'

Josie swallowed and managed to force words out of her suddenly dry mouth. 'Oh…I'm sorry, Dario. I was engrossed in what Signor Costa had to say, and you caught me by surprise.'

'As I see. What's keeping you so busy?' Bringing his horse to a halt, he circled it around while sharing a few words with his estate worker.

'You want to know about the history of this

boundary wall?' he asked Josie when he had finished his conversation.

She nodded, but looking at Dario made it difficult to remember what she *did* want. He looked magnificent, mounted high above her, the reins of his horse in one hand while the other rested loosely on the muscular plane of his thigh.

'Yes—can you help?'

He laughed. 'Not directly. I came over to see if you needed a translator.'

Josie's heart turned a somersault, but she managed to keep her voice under control.

'Thank you, but I can manage,' she replied confidently. Then, afraid of sounding rude, she added, 'I find I can concentrate better without distractions. I…I mean on my own…'

'That's a shame. I was looking forward to watching you at work. It makes a refreshing change. People don't normally come here to do anything constructive. It's a place built for pleasure.'

Josie stifled an involuntary moan. The chances

of getting any work done with Count Dario around were minimal. She would be spending all her time trying not to look at the scenery—and she wasn't thinking about the Tuscan hills...

*What's the matter with me?* She struggled with her conscience. It won in the end—but only just.

'Th...thank you for the offer, Dario, but at the moment I'm just fact-finding for the course I'm designing. I'm sure you'd find it very boring.'

He looked at her, his eyes amused, as though he could see straight through her flimsy defences.

'OK, then. I need to check up on something on the other side of the village anyway, so I'll leave you alone to get on with your work—for the moment, at least.'

He backed his horse to leave. Josie couldn't decide whether she was relieved to be left alone or sorry that he was going.

'Since you've taken the trouble to come all this way to stay in my home, I'll ask around to see if anyone else has some stories about the boundary wall. And come to me when you're ready to see some more of the Castello Sirena's secrets.'

He sounded completely genuine, but the smile she gave him in return was apprehensive.

'That would be great. Thanks.'

Josie had never known herself to be so easily distracted before—*ever*.

*This sort of thing happens to other women, not to me!* she thought. It made her feel weak, which in turn made her feel cross with herself and she scowled.

'Are you sure you're OK?' Dario asked.

'It's the heat, that's all,' she told him abruptly. 'Sun like this is so rare in England, I'm not used to it.'

'Then take care of yourself.' Suddenly his voice was unexpectedly firm. 'Keep to the shade, and always wear a hat. When I see you again, I don't want it to be as a sunstroke victim in the local casualty unit.'

Raising one hand in a salute, he rode away. Josie found herself staring after him and had to apologise to Giacomo, the workman. She didn't need a translation of the workman's reply. His knowing chuckle was enough to give her a pretty good idea of what he was thinking. Blushing furiously, she made a point of turning back to her study of the ancient stones that were being used to repair the wall rather than watch Dario.

*Work first, play later,* she repeated to herself— but for once her usual mantra didn't seem quite so comforting.

Dario couldn't quite put his finger on it, but there was something about Dr Josie Street that unsettled him. He kept thinking about her pale face and tense movements on and off for the rest of the day. She was socially awkward and dressed to disappear into the background rather than make a fashion statement. All the same, he could see why his sister had taken to her—Josie had a charm all of her own. She was delightfully easy to tease, and her innocence was irresistible for someone whose social palate had felt some- what jaded of late. She had been so animated in her conversation with Giacomo. Dario had seen her gestures from a hundred yards away and automatically assumed she needed a translator. It was only as he rode nearer he saw she was simply engrossed in her subject. He liked that. He hadn't been nearly so keen on the way she seemed to lose all her self-confidence when she saw him.

*She went out of her way to communicate with Giacomo, but she could barely string two sentences together once I appeared,* he thought.

For a moment, Dario was reminded of Arietta. He had no idea why, because she had been the complete opposite of Josie—talkative with him, but almost silent in company. Forcibly dismissing the image of his late fiancée, he tried to think of something else. It should have been easy enough. After all, he had lived without Arietta for far longer than they had been together.

But to find her loss could still hurt him acted as a powerful warning.

* * *

*Arietta's memory will* not *be allowed to come back to haunt me again tonight,* Dario thought firmly as he got ready to go out for dinner that evening. As he fastened a pair of solid gold cuff-links into his white dress shirt, he heard the rapid crunch of gravel from outside. Looking out of a window, he saw Josie striding away into the distance, so he strolled out onto his balcony.

'Where are you off to in such a hurry?' he called down to her. 'Can I give you a lift?'

She stopped and turned in a clatter of falling equipment. She was carrying a shuttle tray but it was piled far too high with trowels, brushes and other tools. Now half of them were slithering to the ground.

'Thanks…' she put a hand across her chest as though trying to hide her practical but dull over-alls '…but I couldn't put you to all that trouble…'

'It's no trouble.' He swung back into his suite but, by the time he had pulled on his jacket and made his way down to the courtyard, she was gone.

* * *

Dario kept a lookout for Josie as he drove towards the main gates of his estate a little while
later. When he spotted her, she was already hard
at work beside the old boundary wall. They
waved to each other in passing. That was something; but Dario knew she must have virtually
run like a rabbit to have got there so fast. He
wondered why. There could be nothing scary
about him.

Little scenes with Josie kept edging their way
into his mind all that evening, despite the atten-
tions of several female guests. Unlike Josie, they
were all dressed in the finest clothes that Milan,
Paris and New York had to offer. Everything—
all their glamour, all their charm—was aimed
straight at him. Dario got the same treatment
at every party he attended, so he was used to
it and hardly noticed. Occasionally he allowed
himself to succumb to the flattery, but for some
reason his heart wasn't in it tonight and his mind
started to wander. What sort of dresses might

his new house guest have brought with her? He looked around the assembly, idly imagining Josie dressed in purple silk or black satin. At that point his mind veered off on a very interesting tangent.

*I've got sheets that colour,* he thought. *I wonder what Josie would look like between them.*

Just then a waiter materialised silently at his side. The man was holding a chilled bottle of champagne wrapped in stiff folds of linen.

'No, thanks, I'm driving.' Dario waved him away regretfully, but the interlude put a mischievous thought in his head. He always enjoyed champagne, and kept a good selection of vintages back at the castle.

*I'm sure a glass or two of that would help Josie celebrate her first day at the rock face,* he thought.

Making his excuses to his host, he left and made a rapid escape.

By the end of the day Josie was so tired she could barely put one foot in front of the other, but she could not have been happier. For most of the time she had been alone, which for her made work more relaxing than any holiday. However, in spite of her determination, her mind had kept wandering in the direction of Dario and she needed a rest.

Dragging herself off to bed, she set her alarm very early so she could write up her notes first thing and still be outside before sunrise. The last thing she remembered was the low drone of a powerful engine, cutting through the velvet darkness outside. As she closed her eyes, she remembered the way Dario had described the view from the solar by night and the beautiful turbulence of his expression when he'd looked at her. It was enough to send every other thought clean out of her mind. Drifting off to sleep in her sumptuous empress-sized bed, she smiled. This was a wonderful place, but Dario was full of dangerous temptation for her. The only safe place for an encounter with him would be in her dreams.

By the time his car swung into the courtyard, she was fast asleep.

\* \* \*

Dario leapt out of his car but, before he called for a chauffeur to take it away, he glanced up at the West wing tower. It was in total darkness. That was a blow. Hoping Josie had simply switched off her lights to enjoy the view from the windows as he had suggested, he fetched a bottle of champagne and a couple of glasses. Then he went up and tapped on the door of her suite.

*Never mind. She can still have the full Castello Sirena treatment,* he thought, ignoring his disappointment that he wouldn't be there to share it with her. Scribbling a quick note on the bottle's label, he stood it outside her door.

For some reason he couldn't quite fathom, he wanted to tempt Josie into having a little fun, more than he'd wanted anything for a while. His interrupted dinner party was proof enough. Maybe her resistance was simply a new challenge? Whatever the reason, clearly he wasn't going to be able to get her out of his mind until he'd won her over.

*A long, leisurely lunch should kick things off nicely,* he decided.

Josie was so polite, Dario knew she would never be able to refuse his invitation.

He smiled as he strolled off to bed. It would be deliciously ironic to use her typical English reserve to build bridges between them...

## CHAPTER THREE

Next morning, Josie's alarm woke her before dawn had tinted the sky. The temptation to roll over and snuggle down for another couple of hours was almost overwhelming, but there were a thousand acres of the di Sirena estate waiting to be explored, and she couldn't resist that. Getting ready in double quick time, she flung open the door of her suite, ready to run out and get started—and almost tripped over a bottle of champagne waiting just outside.

*It must have been left over from Dario's wild night out!* She smiled, putting it aside.

Josie hadn't spent a night out—wild or otherwise—for ages. With a twinge of faint embarrassment, she remembered how painful social events like that could be for her.

She slipped out of the castle while the day was

still dim and the air cool. For the next few hours she criss-crossed the di Sirena estate and was soon cursing herself for not bringing a hat. She used pools of shadow wherever she could, but the sun burned hotter by the second.

At first she was so absorbed by her work she had no time to think about anything else. Then she became aware that she was not alone. Wherever she went, Count Dario di Sirena was never far away. She spotted his horse tethered beside the olive press just after she left, then later she saw him approaching the dairy as she was heading away into the hills.

*It's nothing but coincidence,* she thought.

Although coincidence couldn't quite explain the sudden shiver she got every time their paths crossed.

Dario thought that going out for a ride would give him some much needed space and time in his schedule to think. It worked—but not in the way he expected. The still, silent images of Josie observing him from her window, or waving to him as he left home the night before, kept creeping into his mind. He couldn't puzzle out exactly what it was about her that attracted him, but it wasn't for want of opportunity. It seemed that wherever he went today, there she was. She popped up in the most unlikely places, from the hay store to the olive press. After a while it began to make Dario feel slightly uncomfortable. He might have thought he was being stalked, but for one thing. Instead of following him, Josie always managed to be one step ahead. It was as though she was reading his mind and anticipating his movements. He snorted with derision. The idea was ridiculous—but it didn't stop him thinking about it. Usually he was never in any doubt about anything, but Josie was definitely having an effect on him.

From her tightly drawn ponytail right down to the steel toecaps of her sensible work boots, Dr Josie Street meant business. That made her almost unique, in Dario's experience. Her furious blush when he'd explained about the champagne was the closest he got to an unguarded moment, and she barely said a thing even then. It was such a refreshing change from the endless, meaningless chatter poured into his ears at parties every night. Unless something was worth saying Josie kept quiet. Everything about her felt so calm, so stable and so right. So why did she always manage to put him on edge? Dario shook such thoughts away and decided it was definitely time to take command of the situation.

When Josie found herself drawn to a shady glade, she didn't consider there was anything mysterious about it—to begin with. It was simply her desperate need to get out of the heat and dazzling sun. Spotting the glitter of water in a forested depression overlooking the *castello*, she headed straight for it. There wasn't time to enjoy the view as she slithered down a steep rough bank, desperate to reach the cool green depths of the woodland below. Only when she plunged between the gnarled sweet chestnuts, ash trees and birches could she catch her breath and take stock of her surroundings.

As her eyes became accustomed to the cool gloom, a voice drifted through the trees towards her.

*'Ciao, Josie.'*

Dario had looped the reins of his horse over the low branch of a tree and was crouched beside it. He looked like a magnificent animal poised to spring—but in his hand he held a delicate, wide-brimmed straw hat.

'You made me jump!'

'I intended to.' He grinned. 'You didn't take any notice of my warning about sunstroke, so I've come to make you see sense.'

'You seem to appear everywhere I go today,' she said suspiciously.

He stood up and walked towards her, offering the hat.

'I could say the same thing about you. Everywhere I go, you're there ahead of me. I got my staff to look out one of Antonia's hats for you. She won't mind—but I would be very disappointed if you refused this as well as my champagne, Josie.' He smiled.

The sight of Dario dominating the glade was almost enough to rob her of the power of speech. Although he was so tall and well built, he moved almost silently across the forest floor towards her. With his raven dark hair and beautifully honed body accentuated by his white shirt and dark trousers, Josie was reminded again of a panther stalking its prey. Realising what was likely to happen to her resolve if she didn't keep Dario at a distance, she tried to put up a strong defence.

'I notice you're not wearing a hat yourself.' Her voice was uncertain with nerves.

'I'm used to the sun—although you're quite right. Experience isn't a licence to take risks. I make sure I keep to the shade wherever possible, as much for Ferrari's sake as mine.' He tipped his head towards where his bay horse was quietly pulling at some succulent undergrowth. 'I've been exploring these hills all my life, so I know the best places,' he said with a gleam in his eyes. 'For instance, did you know this pool has a secret? We're being watched.'

Crooking his index finger, he beckoned her towards the water's edge.

'When we were children, Antonia used to love being scared by the monster that lives behind that curtain of leaves up there.' He pointed to where greenery hung down over the source of a waterfall tumbling into the pool. 'She used to dare me to pull it back, then she'd run away screaming when I did.'

Josie watched the water splashing down from beneath heavy curtains of fern and ivy. It escaped over bare wet rocks to send ripples dancing out over the clean, clear water.

'There doesn't look to be anything to be scared of.'

Dario chuckled. 'You say that now, but when you're six years old an ancient carved face hidden among the rocks can seem very scary. Local legend says it's Etruscan, but an expert like you would need to check it out to make certain. Antonia has never got around to it.'

Josie's eyes lit up. 'Now you've got me interested.'

'I knew I would.' His smile widened mischievously. 'So—what do you say? Would you dare to come with me now and take a look?'

Josie couldn't answer. She was studying the pool. It had been edged with wide stones, but everything was now worn with age and green with algae. It looked treacherous. Dario was already striding around the perimeter to the other side and calling across the water to her.

'I'll go first. Look, it's perfectly safe—but, if you're nervous, you'll get a better view if you stand over there, beside that nearest alder…'

Josie had dropped her bag and reached his side before he finished speaking. Her fear of being thought not up to a task was greater than her fear of the water, until she saw where she would have to walk. The path to the spring's source was narrow and cut into solid rock. In places, water splashed and played over it as though from a hose.

Edging along, she followed as close behind Dario as she dared. As he crossed the wettest place she took a step forward, felt her foot slip and caught her breath in a tiny cry of panic. Instantly, he grabbed her hand but she had already fought and won the battle to retain her footing. Once again she pulled herself from his grasp.

'I'm fine, thank you.'

Dario wasn't convinced, but grudgingly gave her the benefit of the doubt. 'As long as you're sure.'

'I didn't mean to alarm you. Water just isn't my thing, that's all,' she said, gritting her teeth.

'Does that mean you won't be using the swimming pool down at the *castello* during your stay?' he murmured as they pressed on.

She steeled herself to ignore the interesting tone in his voice.

'Not if I can help it.'

'A shame. Though I, too, much prefer the fun that can be had on dry land.' His words were suggestive, but when Josie glanced at him suspiciously he met her gaze innocently, belying the wickedness she could see in his smile.

'At a time like this I'm inclined to agree with you,' she answered with grim determination as she concentrated on keeping her balance and ignoring the butterflies in her stomach. 'Can you hurry up and show me whatever it is? This is turning into some kind of endurance test!'

'As someone who is in the business of teaching, you should know that nothing good comes without effort.'

'The benefits of hard work can be overstated,' Josie said quietly before she could stop herself.

She had to concentrate grimly on her footwork, but Dario could afford to look at her quizzically.

'What do you mean?'

Josie cursed the twin distractions of Etruscan art and the slippery surface. She had said too much. Furious with herself for accidentally bringing up such a sensitive subject, she tried to laugh it off.

'Oh…while I was studying, my boyfriend found someone else to catalogue his artefacts for him. You know how it is,' she finished lamely, expecting him to laugh.

He didn't. Instead, he looked at her for a quiet moment, while Josie shivered under his leisurely, assessing gaze.

'What a foolish man, not to see what he had,' he said quietly, before turning away as if the compliment had never happened. Josie took a deep breath, trying to control the adrenalin suddenly fizzing through her veins.

'Here we are…careful…now look at this…'

Reaching out, Dario pushed aside the curtain of young hart's tongue fronds. Nourished by the run off from the slopes above, they were easily two feet long and covered the source of the waterfall with thick green ripples. As he moved the leaves apart, Josie saw that the water poured out from the mouth of a hideous grinning mask. It must have truly terrified Antonia when she'd played here as a child, more than twenty years before.

'Wow!' she breathed.

In her excitement she forgot all her fears about the slippery surface. Squeezing in front of Dario, she leaned forward for a closer look. At that moment a wren burst out indignantly from its hiding place behind the stone head. Whirring past Josie's face, it missed her by inches and gave her such a fright she jumped, lost her footing—and toppled straight into the pool.

Her world exploded in a mass of bubbles. Before she had time to realise what was happening, she was grabbed and pulled above the surface again. Half drowned and spluttering, she found herself held tightly in Dario's arms. She felt his body shaking and heard his laughter, but her indignation died as she discovered how incredible it felt to be pressed against his hard, unyielding body.

She stopped struggling. For one glorious moment the glade fell still and silent. All she could hear was the sound of her own heartbeat and feel Dario's pulse beating in time with hers. It was intoxicating, and such a primal feeling. His beautiful face was so close, she felt her lips part in anticipation of something so wonderful she dared not give it a name.

Then she remembered what it felt like when temptation led to betrayal. Panic engulfed her. In a surge of desperation, she tried to wriggle from his grasp, flailing the water into a maelstrom.

'Hold still!'

Josie stopped splashing. Her feet floated down and she found her toes brushing the floor of the pool.

'Oh…' she moaned, feeling a complete fool.

'You're quite safe with me,' he said reassuringly, and Josie wanted to believe it.

She tipped her head back to look at him properly. Water trickling over the carved intensity of his face sparkled in golden streaks of sunlight flickering through the trees.

'Oh, dear—you seem to have got a faceful of water!' She blushed. 'I'm so sorry.'

Dario said nothing. His white shirt was plastered against his chest, showing dark shadows of hair beneath. Feeling his body, so hot and vital in the cool seductive depths of the pool, Josie unconsciously relaxed against him. Her whole body felt as liquid as the water, ready to absorb him and flow around him for ever. His eyes feasted on her face, and it was the ultimate aphrodisiac. When his hands began to move, she held her breath in an agony of expectation. As he gently brushed a lock of wet hair away from the corner of her mouth, she closed her eyes again. Unable to resist, she parted her lips and this time she knew exactly what she wanted. Her breathing quickened in desperate anticipation of his kiss.

Then, at the last moment, either her common sense returned or her nerve failed her—she never knew which it was. Opening her eyes, she shook her head so quickly and violently that droplets of water flew through the air like shards of glass. Letting go of his supportive hand, she waded away from him and towards the edge of the pool. There, she hauled herself out of the water and began to walk away, back to where her things lay scattered on the forest floor. She had never felt so tempted by a man before in her life. She knew she had to put some distance between them as soon as possible, for the sake of her own sanity.

Still waist-deep in the water, Dario surveyed her like Neptune.

'You should be more careful.'

'I know—that's why I got out of there as soon as I could,' Josie snapped. 'I'll be keeping well away from the edge from now on, believe me.'

*In every sense of the word,* she added silently.

The thought of Dario leaping in to save her

again if she got into difficulties was doing very strange things to her body.

Dario hardly heard what she said. Josie amazed him. Not many people were prepared to stand up to him. Now, soaked to the skin and with her wet white T-shirt clinging to her body in almost transparent folds, she was a breathtaking sight.

Acutely aware of his scrutiny, Josie kept on walking away from him, trying to wring the water out of her clothes and ponytail as she did so.

'And please don't look at me like that.'

'Have you got eyes in the back of your head?'

'I don't need them, where you're concerned. I can feel you looking at me.'

'It's meant as a compliment,' he mused.

'Then thank you, but please stop,' she said sharply. 'I'd like to get a photograph of that spring. It's exactly the sort of thing I'm interested in. If you really do want to help me, Dario, you could tell me if there are any more hidden treasures like that one on your estate.'

She could already feel the heat of the day pulling the moisture out of her cheap, thin clothes. If she blushed much more, they would be drying out from the inside as well as the outside. Trying to ignore the sounds behind her of Dario stripping off his sodden shirt, she knelt on the forest floor. Emptying the contents of her messenger bag onto the soft green moss surrounding the pool, she picked out her camera.

'You should come out here in the sunshine with me. You'll get dry quicker,' Dario called.

Before she could stop herself, Josie looked up and saw him in magnificent silhouette. He was rubbing some still-dry parts of his shirt over his wet body before sliding his arms into its damp embrace again. 'It's a great way to cool off, but when I decided to treat you to lunch out here I never expected to need towels as well.'

'Lunch?'

'You don't think I'd come out to find you without being fully prepared?' He strolled across the glade, doing up the buttons of his shirt as he walked. Josie purposely avoided watching the way his fingers moved, as it brought back all too clearly the memory of their potent strength. Instead, she looked him straight in the face—but that laid her wide open to the devastating effect of his smile.

Holding Josie powerless in his arms had aroused all sorts of feelings in Dario. Now, he couldn't stop thinking about the best use for secluded glades—and that was seduction. When he had ridden out here to surprise her with an impromptu picnic, he hadn't expected to end up holding her so tightly against his body, even in the role of lifeguard. Dario was a typical red-blooded Italian male and found it difficult to ignore temptation. Especially when it came in the form of a voluptuous woman in thin, wet clothing.

\* \* \*

As Dario raised his arm to unstrap the picnic basket from his horse's saddle, his white sleeve flickered brightly against the mysterious depths of the wood. It was as good as a signal to Josie. She tensed as he walked back to join her.

'Hmm…as I thought—the staff have only packed hand towels, although if I put this picnic rug around your shoulders—'

The rug was folded up so tightly he needed both hands to shake it free. Unfurling it, he moved forward to swirl it around Josie's shoulders, but when he touched her she drew in her breath and backed away.

'I can manage, thank you.' Reaching out, she snatched the picnic rug from his fingers.

'You're shivering. Let's go and sit in that patch of sunshine over there.'

Picking up the picnic basket, he went over to the far side of the clearing. When he looked back she was following, but slowly and at a distance. Dario smiled to himself; he had enough experience to know when a woman was nearly his.

He started to unpack the things he had brought, then sat back on his heels as she came towards him cautiously.

'The archaeology isn't suddenly going to disappear before you can get to it, and I'm hardly going to eat you when my kitchen has provided us with all *this*.' He spread a hand towards the tempting display he was setting out. 'Why not take the time actually to enjoy yourself for once, Josie? Are you too sensible to relax? Give it a try over lunch—there's no one here to see!'

Unable to resist his challenge, as he'd known she would be, she sat down, but several feet away from him. When Dario went back to his work without comment, she eventually leaned forward to help. Without moving his head, he saw her hands moving in and out of his peripheral vision, arranging pristine white crockery like clouds against the sky-blue picnic cloth.

'There. What could be better than that?' He turned to her.

For a split second they looked into each other's

eyes, then her glance slipped away to the half a dozen tempting types of antipasto the *castello*'s kitchen had packed for them. As the pool of sunlight gilded her wet brown hair, Dario opened a bottle of limoncello and poured a shot of it into each of two crystal glasses. Topping them up with chilled mineral water, he handed one to Josie. Then, touching his glass lightly against hers, he said softly, *'Salute!'*

She gazed at him, then at the food on display, and then at the drink in her hand.

'You did all this for me?' Her tone was one of sheer disbelief.

'Where I come from, picnics are a couple of rounds of sandwiches grabbed from a supermarket. I don't know what to say...or where to start...' she began, but Dario didn't need to be told—the look in her eyes said it all. He moved around, away from the sudden rush of emotion he felt at her obvious pleasure, until he was on the far side of their feast. From there, safely back in seduction mode, he started to offer her little dishes of *caponata* and pasta salad, smiling as she gave in to temptation.

Josie chose some roasted tomatoes and peppers, gleaming with the estate's own olive oil, mozzarella and a slice of fragrant focaccia spiked with rosemary and crystals of sea salt. While Dario loaded his plate with a little of everything on display, she watched him covertly. His movements had the smooth assurance of a man born to lead. With another shiver, she noticed the strength in his smooth brown forearms. The sleeves of his shirt were turned back, showing off his taut muscles. That provoked a reaction deeper than anything her ex-fiancé had ever sown in her. Unexpected sensations simmered within her, and they were scary—not because Dario felt threatening, but because of the way her body responded so easily to his. She could remember every nuance of feeling aroused by his capable hands as they rescued her from the water. Her body had been without the touch of a man for so long, she had forgotten how exciting the slightest contact could be.

'Is there anything else you'd like, Josie?'

In her heightened state, his voice was a purr of encouragement as seductive as the sound of the golden orioles warbling deep in the woodland around them. She felt her mouth go dry. Her whole body began to melt under the warmth of his gaze. To hide her growing arousal, she took a long, slow sip of her limoncello. Nothing in her life so far had prepared her for the sensuous promise she heard in Dario's voice—or the primitive reactions of her body. The lilt of his rich accent cast a magical spell over her every time he spoke her name.

*This is seduction by telepathy,* she thought.

Dario seemed perfectly attuned to her, and her physical response to his confident masculinity. Her body turned to water beneath his gaze, ebbing and flowing like the warm flush that threatened to engulf her entirely. It was a struggle to conceal the effect he was having on her. Before they met, she had assumed any contact with this man would be brief and boring. Now his silent temptation threatened to undermine all her good intentions to concentrate on her work while she had the chance.

'Let me guess. Before you got here, you had already assumed you would dislike me on sight. Now you find I'm not the man you expected. Isn't that so?' he said quietly.

Josie swallowed her reply. It would only incriminate her, when her expression alone was enough to set the light of amusement dancing in his amazing eyes.

'And now you are wondering how I know that! It's because I thought exactly the same about you, Josie. To begin with.'

She picked up her cutlery, pretending to be more interested in her meal than she was in Dario. It was a mistake. She might be able to ignore the tremors of excitement powering through her body but it was impossible to suppress the way her hands were trembling. Sunlight filtering between the leaves high above flickered and danced over her silver fork, betraying her.

'You're making me nervous,' she announced in her defence.

'Really? I don't know why. It's never been my intention to scare you.'

'I didn't say I was scared. It's more a kind of… passive intimidation…' she managed. The past histories of her mother, her best friend and her own broken engagement were powerful reminders of what could happen when a man didn't get things his own way, but right now defiance was the last thing on Josie's mind.

Dario's beautifully sculpted mouth lifted in a smile. 'I imagine my forebears would be pleased to hear you say that. They ruled by the sword. But, speaking for myself, I've never liked to think I make people nervous. I want you to enjoy yourself, Josie. So…what more can I do to please you?'

The tempting lilt in his voice was deliberately ambiguous. She could see it in his eloquent dark eyes.

'I think this lovely lunch is enough for the time being, thank you,' she told him unsteadily.

He nodded, and turned his attention to his own plate.

Josie felt a sudden stab of disappointment that he had taken her words as a hint to back off.

'What keeps a man like you buried out here in the countryside?' she said, desperate to steer the topic of conversation away from herself. As she moved, a mischievous little breeze cooled the damp T-shirt beneath the blanket around her shoulders. It clung to the smooth curves of her breasts, sharpening her nipples into almost painful points. They were tingling in a way that made her want to learn a whole lot more about Dario, despite all her reservations.

'I can't tear myself away from the place.' He raised both his hands in a gesture of resignation. 'This estate, these people—they are my duty but, beyond that, this countryside is part of me. Although I couldn't expect a modern woman to understand this.'

Josie stiffened. '*Modern?* What's that supposed to mean? Are you making fun of me?'

Dario turned his attention to a pile of fruit that stood between them. Selecting a perfect peach, he cupped it in one hand, feeling its mass and appreciating its weight.

'The meaning I had in mind was *intellectual*,' he said idly. 'You're used to using your mind instead of taking simple pleasure from your surroundings. You've come here from a place where learning is prized above emotion, and so that has coloured your attitude.'

'I sometimes wish it hadn't,' she said wistfully.

He smiled. It was a slow, seductive gesture that reached right out to her.

'Good…because here at the Castello Sirena, emotions run deep; deeper even than the spring that feeds our ancient pool. It is a place made for pleasure, not for relentless work. Let me show you.' His voice was a warm caress of desire. 'In my world, even the simple acting of eating can be transformed into a beautiful experience.'

Taking a silver fruit knife, he cut a neat segment from the fruit in his other hand. Reaching across their picnic, he held the slice out to her.

Josie's mind went to pieces completely.

*Work later, play now...*

The gentle sounds of nature receded as her head filled with clouds of cotton wool. She seemed to be looking at herself from outside. Instead of taking the piece of fruit from Dario's fingers with her own, she watched herself lean forward to take it directly into her mouth. Through a warm mist of arousal, she heard herself gasp as the peach's rich nectar ran down her chin.

Dario had never expected her to do something so spontaneous. His shock and surprise seamlessly turned to raw lust, ready to overwhelm him. No one could expect a man like Count Dario di Sirena to refuse such an invitation. Swiftly and silently, he took Josie's hands and moved in to taste her.

# CHAPTER FOUR

FOR endless moments Josie was powerless to resist Dario's sudden onslaught. The tip of his tongue traced delicately over her skin until she willed him to pull her into his arms and make mad passionate love to her…

…Then a sudden breeze rustling through the trees startled her out of her paralysis. Shrinking away from him, she stood up, but he followed. Josie had been so completely lost in the moment, she was still holding his hand. There was no point in trying to let go now—her body wouldn't allow it. When he took a step forward to claim her again, she succumbed to the magic of his mouth a second time.

Josie knew she should resist, but it was as though their kisses were always meant to be. As his arms enfolded her, she melted under their firm pressure. The touch of his fingers as they glided over her back pressed her wet T-shirt against her naked skin. When she shivered he held her closer, but she wasn't cold. The heat of desire kept rising and building within her until she twined her arms around his neck. This was it—she was ready to be released from her long and painful sentence of self-denial. All the years of loneliness would slip away, forgotten, in this single supreme act. She pressed her body against his, feeling the scarily exciting kick of his manhood against her belly. When that happened he drew back, and for the first time in what felt like heady hours of excitement their lips parted.

Dario's chest rose and fell rapidly as he snatched at steadying breaths. Josie fought the urge to lean forward and kiss him again—and for one desperate moment she saw him struggle with that same primitive need. Then he closed his eyes and his head sank until his forehead rested against hers. For one heart-stopping moment she thought he was going to take her lips again.

'Yes...' she breathed in reply, not wanting him to stop. His response was a sigh almost absorbed by the silence. 'Please, Dario...'

After all, as he had said, there was no one about to see...and no one but Josie's conscience to know what happened out here among the trees. Her mind had tortured her for too long already. Rising on tiptoe, she searched for his lips with her own and tasted his skin.

All the time her hands roamed over his body, he stood as still as stone. It was only when her hands slid around his waist that he stirred and gave a wordless moan of longing and regret. Then he reached around and grasped her wrists. That one simple movement woke Josie from her trance. With a spasm of alarm, she realised how close she had come to total surrender. She stood back and stared at him, shocked.

Dario's expression was a mask of regret, his

eyes squeezed shut as he whispered, 'No...I can't... I'm sorry...*Arietta*...'

Josie's longing drained away, replaced by the old, familiar mix of anger, shame and humili-ation.

'You could at least call me by the right name!' she spat.

That broke the spell.

'I should never have done anything at all,' he said grimly, dropping her hands and striding away across the glade towards his horse.

Josie watched him go in silent horror. If only she had trusted her instincts. For years, she had been careful to stay out of harm's way. On that principle, she should have kept right away from Dario. She had suspected there must be a girl in his life, and now she knew—*and no wonder,* she added, *he's irresistible!*

Instantly, she regretted the terrible thought. It catapulted her straight back to the dark, awful moment when she'd discovered Andy had been cheating on her. Back then, she hadn't been able to understand how any woman could inflict such agony on another and here she was, guilty of almost exactly the same thing.

*I've always said I couldn't bear to put anyone through what I've suffered,* she thought. *Not even for a man with kisses like that...*

She had to get away. Snatching up her bag and camera, she plunged out of the glade and into the sunshine. The thought of investigating that fountainhead now made her feel sick with guilt. It would always be linked in her mind with the first time Dario had touched her, and where that wonderful sensation had led.

*If I hadn't succumbed to him, hadn't* encouraged *him, if he hadn't moved in on me...*

Desperate for distraction, she scrambled back up the slope, away from that seductively shady woodland glade. The sun beat down mercilessly and she had left the sun hat behind. Tough, dry grasses scratched at her hands and the dusty hot air kept catching in her throat. By the time she reached the crest of the hill, her breath was tearing holes in her chest but she still couldn't forget the feel of Dario's hands and the exciting insistence of his lips.

Dropping to the ground in the meagre shade of a juniper, she looked down on the scene she had left behind. Dario had returned to the woodland edge. He was half in shadow, half in sunlight. Shielding her eyes against the sun, she studied him. His hands were on his hips and he was staring up the hill towards her. As she watched, waiting for him to jeer at her, he did something quite unexpected. His head dropped, he rubbed his hands over his face as if trying to scrub off something dirty—and then he turned away.

It was an indignity too far.

Josie was only too aware that she used work as an excuse to retreat from real life. *And this is why!* she thought furiously. *Is it any wonder I keep myself to myself when there are men like Dario about?*

She took out her notebook and looked around

for something new to study, determined to try to carry on as normal. It was hopeless. She could only think of one thing, and it wasn't work.

It seemed to Josie that whenever she tried to taste life as other people lived it, she came unstuck. She had started off her adult life by using hard work as the measure of her success. By the time she had realised her fiancé was more interested in his own prospects than their future together, he was already having an affair with one of her colleagues. That betrayal had been awful, and public. But there was another, darker side to her disappointment. The idea that sex with Andy had never set her on fire had been a private worry, which made today ten times more painful. In a few seconds Dario had blown away all her fears of being frigid, and released the animal inside her. Now she found herself wanting more. A man who could surely have any woman he wanted had managed to unravel all her self-control simply by holding her in his arms. In the seductive shadows, that scared her. Out here in the brutal light of day, it stoked her anger. It took the sight of Dario's reaction to provoke an emotion in her more powerful than the fear of her own needs.

*No one turns their back on me any more!* she thought, getting to her feet and brushing her hands free from dust in a gesture dramatic enough for him to see. Shaking out the folds of her damp T-shirt and jabbing all the escaped strands of soggy hair behind her ears, she took a deep breath. Then she marched down the slope again. In a few frantic moments she had learned a little about Dario di Sirena—but a whole lot more about herself.

It was time to start being ruthlessly honest. He had kissed her only after she had first accepted his offer of a picnic in a secluded spot.

*So what else did I expect to happen, after that clinch in the pool?*

The man had acted completely in character. In

contrast, she had sent her common sense back home to England!

*A simple 'no thank you' to the picnic would probably have done the trick. I should have tried that first,* she told herself, but knew it would have been impossible. Well, now she had to face up to the consequences of her actions.

The sun pounded down on her head almost as fiercely as the blood pulsed in her ears. Josie now realised she had been secretly wondering what it would be like to be kissed by Dario since first setting eyes on his sensuous mouth and those wonderfully dark, expressive eyes.

It was time to put her willpower to the test. Officially she was here to work, and that would be so much easier with Dario's goodwill rather than his contempt.

*I'm bigger than my shame, master of my anger, even stronger than the lust that's still running through me—and this will prove it!* she thought, stamping the seal on her determination with every step. The slope gave her a bit more momentum than she expected.

Dario was adjusting the harness of his horse, ready to leave the scene of the disaster. When he heard a noise and turned back to see what was happening, Josie was half-jogging down the hill in order to keep her balance.

'I hope you don't think I'm running back to you,' she said with all the dignity she could scrape together.

'No. But I do hope you have come back to accept my apology,' he said gravely, picking up her discarded sun hat and holding it out to her.

Josie hesitated, unable to decide whether he was being sincere or simply laughing at her. Stiffening her resolve, she grabbed the hat. To show how mad she was at him, she jammed it firmly onto her head. It was only then she realised Antonia's head must be bigger than her own. The sun hat came right down over her eyes, only stopping when it lodged on her ears.

Before she could do anything about it, lean

brown fingers intruded into her restricted field of vision. Dario tilted the brim so he could look straight down into her eyes.

'That's better. As I said, you should never go without a hat in this sun.'

His tone was as cool as a mountain stream, in stark contrast to the liquid heat of his kisses only moments ago. There was no trace of emotion visible in him now, either good or bad. Angry though she was, Josie felt her knees turn to jelly again beneath his penetrating gaze.

'I shouldn't have behaved like that,' she said, hotly conscious of his scrutiny.

'Neither should I.'

He took a couple of careful steps back, putting a discreet distance between them again, before continuing unevenly, 'And then I made things worse by calling you by the wrong name. I apologise.' He cleared his throat, then continued with obvious reluctance. 'Arietta was my fiancée. She died some time ago. There was an accident—'

He stopped. She saw him take a deep breath and steady himself.

'I thought I had put the episode behind me, but apparently not.'

Josie stared at him, making her face a mask. She had to—her whole body was alive with uncertainty again. She knew all about loss, but it seemed Dario had suffered a far worse disaster than her own.

'I…I understand. I'm sorry, too. It was just as much my fault as yours. I shouldn't have led you on, Dario. We both got carried away. That's all.'

He nodded his appreciation, then cleared his throat again. 'It took a lot of courage to come back here after what happened, Josie.'

He was right, but she had never expected him to acknowledge that.

'I learned a long time ago that running away never solved anything, so now I just try to learn from my mistakes. I won't make the same one twice,' she said, trying to defuse the situation.

'No, I can't imagine you would,' he said drily.

\* \* \*

From the far side of the glade came the sound of his horse, which had wandered off and was now fretting with its bit.

*I must be mad,* she thought. *Straight after kissing him like some sort of harlot, I've swung back to acting like a boring old maid!*

His kiss had made her feel like a woman again for the first time in years. She had forgotten how good that sensation could be, and she wanted to experience it again. Soon. She dithered, blushing, and not knowing what to say.

*If I told you what I was really thinking, it would be 'goodbye research, hello disaster!'* she thought.

'In which case, I'll leave you to get on with your work and say *arrivederci*—for now.'

As Dario turned to walk away, Josie felt a powerful urge to call him back. He anticipated her. Swinging himself up into his saddle, he turned his horse in a wide arc, passing very close to where she stood. He treated her to a long, lingering view of his tight breeches and enviable seat as he circled the glade.

Lifting the corners of his mouth in a smile, he acknowledged their new intimacy. 'But the next time your schedule allows you some room to do something scarily spontaneous again, Josie, be sure to let me know.'

Nudging his horse into a canter, he headed out of the glade and off across the grassy hillside.

Josie was left to stare after him. The way Dario had coaxed her into baring her soul to him was uncanny. She might have expected to feel angry that he found her so easy to read. Instead, she felt let down and strangely empty inside. The wonderful warmth of arousal he had coaxed into life deep within her body threatened to fade as she watched him ride away.

But it didn't die completely—and, since tasting the temptation of his kiss, Josie knew it never would.

# CHAPTER FIVE

DARIO didn't look back. He rode fast, straight back to the stables. There he leapt off his horse and let the stallion find his own way to the nearest stable lad. Dario's favourite refuge in times of crisis was his art. Striding straight for his studio in the *castello* grounds, he went in and slammed the door. Leaning back heavily against it, he tried to think. Since Arietta died, he had roamed from woman to woman, picking, choosing, but never staying with anyone for long. To do anything else was unthinkable. He always slipped away before emotion could coil him in its oily grasp. Other people might envy him, but they only saw his free and easy attitude. Casual charm was his mask of choice.

Until now, he had never cared what other people thought. He had gone out each day with a smile on his face, and that was enough to reassure most people that he was happy. Now the sunlight had shone into more than that secluded glade. It had thrown back the shadows from the most private place inside him. It was somewhere so dark, not even Dario was aware of how deep its secrets went. All he knew was that this morning he had let his nonchalant shield slip. So what was different about today?

*Dr Josie Street,* he thought.

Their kisses had torn away everything; he'd been captured by the simple pleasure of that moment, of that woman, in a way he hadn't experienced in years. Raw, naked lust had risen up, overwhelming all his finer feelings and making him almost lose control. Shame burnt through him—for a moment he'd forgotten Arietta.

When Josie had stormed away after their spectacular kiss, Dario had found himself unable to follow her. Instead, he had let out a stream of curses. He had enjoyed many women since losing Arietta, so what had happened today to make him say *her* name out loud?

Maybe it was because Josie was so different from all those other women. She had something they lacked. For a start, she might appear composed and serious, but he sensed that deeper down there was a core of fire. The women who usually competed for his attention never hid their passion. They tried to use it as bait. Josie fought to hide hers every inch of the way.

*In that respect we're alike,* he thought with a jolt of recognition. Most of the time she coped by staying silent, but that would never work on him again—not after he had felt the heat of her response and the passion of her kisses. Those few incendiary moments had unleashed the tigress in her, but instinctively Dario knew that if he casually took advantage of her awakened passion then Josie would never forgive herself. Or him.

There was another reason why he held back, too. Time had dimmed Arietta's memory but, for some reason, it had burst back into life when he'd responded to Josie. She attracted him in a way that no other woman had since Arietta, but he had no desire to go through that much pain again. And he suspected that if he pursued Josie, that was exactly what would happen.

For the rest of the day, Josie could think of nothing but Dario's kiss and the feel of his body. As she worked her way around the grounds of the Castello Sirena, her senses were tuned to detect him. Every moment she spent practising her Italian with the farm workers and villagers, she was secretly wondering about Dario—where he was and what he was doing.

Later, when she retreated to her room to write up her notes, she finally found out. As the shadows lengthened, the growl of a high-performance engine passed beneath her window. Looking out, she saw a beautiful royal-blue sports car accelerate away down the lime avenue.

That told her Dario's take on their encounter was very different from her own.

He must have put her out of his mind already. He was going back out on the town.

The next few days were a horrible mixture of routine and denial for Josie. Her mind kept telling her to forget about Dario. Her body had different ideas. Each time she thought of him, her pulse ran riot. She coped in the only way she knew how, by drawing up a punishing schedule of surveying and study for every day of her projected stay. She ticked tasks off that 'to do' list like a metronome. Every evening she fell into her dreamily comfortable bed, satisfied with what she had achieved. It was a routine that had got her top marks for as long as she could remember. It also shielded her bruised heart and kept a tight lid on her newly discovered libido. But soon her emotions fought against being confined any longer. The moment she closed her eyes, images of Dario filled her mind. The sound of his sports car roaring away as he set off on another night of pleasure made her pictures of him still more vivid. She could almost feel his hands around her waist, his cheek brushing her hair and his long, lingering kisses setting her senses on fire all over again…

She tried to tell herself he was a distraction she couldn't afford. That might have worked for her after Andy left, but it sure as hell didn't work with Dario.

Although their paths had somehow stopped crossing after their encounter in the wood, Josie wanted Dario to know it was because she was working, and not just hiding away from him. Whenever she was out on the estate she tried to forget him, but spent half her time looking over her shoulder. She was as wary as a gazelle on the African plains, on the alert for the lion that might pounce at any time.

As time went on and he didn't appear, she began to settle back into her normal routine, managing, for the most part, to push her frustrated desires back into hiding—and then one evening Dario rode out of the sunset while she was busy brushing the fine, dry soil away from her latest find. From being lost in her thoughts, Josie was thrown into confusion. With desperate movements she stood up, shoving her hair behind her ears and brushing the worst of the dust from the legs of her overalls. Then she rubbed her sleeve over her brow, before realising it was as grimy as her knees had been. Desperately she grabbed the towel from the table where she washed her finds. Without a mirror, she had to hope it made any smudges better and not worse. Trying to look absorbed in her work for the agonising minutes it took him to ride up to her was impossible. It was only when she stopped trying that he smiled.

'Dario,' she greeted him quietly.

'Josie,' he replied in kind as he jumped down from his horse.

Despite her apprehension, she couldn't help checking his saddle for another picnic basket. There wasn't one.

'I wondered what you were doing here,' she said to cover her embarrassment when he noticed what she was looking at.

'I live here, remember?'

'When you aren't roaring around the countryside by night,' she said before she could stop herself.

He raised his eyebrows, strolling past her to investigate her finds table. 'You noticed?'

'I can't help it…er…because the sound of your engine disturbs my work every night, that is.'

'But your suite is always in darkness,' he said casually, picking up one of her site sketches. 'I'm here to deliver a message, by the way. I thought you'd like to know that Antonia rang— she's coming home tomorrow. Hmm…I like this drawing. It's artistic as well as being accurate. You're clearly a woman of many talents.'

Josie tried not to feel smug, but it didn't work. In the face of his obvious appreciation, she felt horribly tongue-tied.

'You learn to be a jack of all trades in this job,'

she muttered. 'Art used to be a bit of a hobby of mine. Not that I ever get a chance to do anything about it these days, apart from site sketches,' she said wistfully.

He made a disapproving noise. 'Have you ever thought of working some of these drawings up into full-sized paintings? They would add something unique to your coursework.'

'It's tempting…' she said, stealing a long look at his beautiful profile as he studied her work, '…but there's no point. Effort like that would be wasted on the academics who read my stuff.'

'Come on, Josie—don't be so defeatist! You're a highly qualified woman with a lot of talent, both inside and outside of your usual sphere. Why be content with such a small market for your skills?'

'You sound very sure of yourself. Who's to say anybody else would share your opinion?'

'I've studied art for long enough to know good work when I see it—you should have more confidence in yourself!'

His voice tailed off, as though he'd just heard his own enthusiasm. Josie glanced at him, but he looked away at almost the same instant. She almost caught herself smiling. According to Antonia, her brother Dario was a famous seducer but, standing in front of her now, he looked completely lost for words.

His uncomfortable silence didn't last long; he seemed to gather himself and carried on in a more practical manner. 'With artistic talent like this, you could draw in a much wider audience. Quality artwork would attract people who wouldn't normally think of picking up an archaeology textbook. Me, for one.'

Josie chewed her lip. 'Do you really think so?'

'Definitely. I'm certain others would think that way, too.'

He sounded genuine, and smiled to drive the point straight into her heart. The memory of their eventful picnic made Josie break eye contact and move away from him. She started to tap a pile of already tidy papers into a meticulously rectangular block.

'Oh, I don't know. I don't have the time, or the equipment...'

'You should *make* time. It counts as work, so you wouldn't have to feel it's being wasted,' Dario said in a voice that gave her no option. 'And, as for equipment, that's no excuse either. I keep a well-stocked studio. Anything you want, you can get from me. In a purely artistic sense, of course,' he added hurriedly, seeing her frown.

'It's very kind, Dario, but I really can't spare the time...'

She looked over towards the Roman hearth she was uncovering, stone by stone. It was long, knee-numbing stuff.

He dropped his voice to a conspiratorial whisper. 'Come on...you know you want to! That floor has waited two thousand years for you to come along with your trowel and brush. Light and landscape is something that must be captured when it happens, and while it lasts. Like happiness, and laughter,' he added.

When she smiled, he suddenly reached out to her. She flinched, and his fingers stopped short of making contact with her cheek. She took a step back, leaving his hand to fall back to his side.

'I can see you've fully recovered from…the heat,' he said with a brittle smile. 'In which case, as I've done what I came to do, I'll leave you to your work. Goodbye, Josie, but don't forget what I said. Capture the moment. If you wait too long, it will slip through your fingers. And you'll always regret missing out.'

'You sound very sure about that!' She chuckled, but all signs of amusement had vanished from his expression.

'I am. Life can deal anyone a bad hand, Josie. Work is a great refuge, but you need to keep it in proportion. Look at me—running this estate and making sure I can pass it on to little Fabio in good heart takes up a lot of time, and it used to be that I'd focus only on that—but it's no way to live.'

'Fabio? But he's not your son.' Josie picked up on the name but then put her hand to her mouth. 'I'm sorry; it's none of my business.'

He looked startled, but hid it quickly. 'You're so close to Antonia, I assumed you knew all about that already.'

'We spend most of our time chatting about work,' Josie said. 'At least we did, until Fabio came along. We hardly ever talk about our families.'

He shrugged. 'I simply assumed she would have filled you in.'

'Dario, I don't need to be told anything more about you than I know already, unless you'd like me to know something,' she said, while secretly hoping he would insist on revealing more.

He was silent, seeming to struggle with his thoughts for a moment before the mask came down and, to Josie's disappointment, he was once again the suave, charming playboy.

'You're right. We both have work to do, so I'll let you get back into your trench,' he said smoothly, before mounting his horse and cantering quickly back the way he had come.

From then on, Josie couldn't stop wondering why Dario had made his little nephew his heir. Dario was only a few years older than she was. What made him so sure, so young, that he would never have children of his own? Was it something to do with his mysterious dead fiancée? Josie wasn't sure she wanted to find out the answer, but his words nagged at her like a puzzle begging to be solved.

She was tortured with curiosity for the rest of the day, but her worst moment came that night as she was drifting off to sleep, when the sound of his high-powered car dragged her awake again. Every night it took him away, leaving her sleepless and alone.

Dario and the memory of his kisses had awoken a need in Josie that would not let her rest.

She got out of bed and went over to the window to watch the tail-lights of his car speeding away down the long lime avenue. Dario was heading off towards the city, with all its temptations and distractions. He had a million friends. His social life was so full he need never be alone, but something about him made Josie think that, secretly, he might be as lonely as she was.

Josie's curiosity kept her awake until she heard Dario return in the early hours. Her lack of sleep meant she woke up late the next morning, which put her in a foul mood from the beginning. She knew from experience that she would never catch up on the lost time. She was also half-afraid Dario might have taken her words to heart and brought a conquest home to prove a point. She found herself angry for caring so much about it, but she needn't have worried. The *castello* and its estate were both practically deserted as she walked the half mile to her excavation beside the old olive press. She worked away at uncovering the ancient flagstone hearth until the sun was high in the sky. Then she heard the sound of a car. It was one of the di Sirena limousines, and it sighed to a halt at the junction between the main drive and the drove road.

'Josie! Look what we've got for you!' a familiar voice called out.

Josie stood up to see her friend Antonia erupting from the car's back seat and galloping along the track towards her, swinging several paper carrier bags. Plump and pretty, Toni had the enthusiasm of a puppy but was out of breath in seconds. Jumping out of her trench, Josie ran to meet her. Taking the bag, she peered inside.

'An orange bikini?' She goggled. 'That's the very last thing I would have guessed!'

'Dario said you needed one.' Antonia was grinning from ear to ear. 'He says you've got to learn to swim.'

'If I got into a swimming pool with your brother while I was wearing this, I think drowning would be the least of my worries,' Josie said drily.

'You're all right. You'd be perfectly safe.'

Josie laughed. 'Oh, dear. And people say *I'm* unworldly! Hey—it looks like your mothering skills have gone a bit haywire…' she said, craning past Antonia to check the deserted back seat of the limousine. 'You've *never* left Fabio back in Rimini?'

'Of course not, silly! Dario was waiting for us by the gate on his horse, Ferrari. He had brought one of Fabio's ponies out with him so they could ride home together.'

'*One* of his ponies? How many does that child have?' Josie asked in astonishment.

Antonia rolled her big brown eyes in a gesture so reminiscent of Dario, Josie was touched. She smiled.

'I have no idea. Dario likes him to have the right size, so we have a selection here.' Antonia smiled a bit guiltily. 'Money might not buy happiness, but it makes most problems go away.'

She hesitated for a moment, as if lost in thought. After a pause, she shook herself and elbowed Josie in the ribs again, grinning. 'So you're still on speaking terms with Dario, then? He never said.'

'Why would he? I'm just a guest here.' Josie laughed, but jumped back into her trench before Antonia could see her expression.

'Then you can have a great time getting to know him better at the party tomorrow,' Antonia replied airily. 'Dario's decided he's going to use it as an excuse to celebrate our safe return from Rimini. He's invited everyone we know and a few more besides, so it'll be brilliant. But then, Dario's parties always are.'

'Thank goodness I shall be safely tucked up in bed long before that.'

Antonia frowned. 'Oh, come on, Josie! I know you aren't the sociable type, but couldn't you make an exception just this once? It'll be fun. There are usually all sorts of things going on— an auction of promises, and games—'

Josie grimaced.

'Don't look like that. It's all in aid of charity and you'll love it, really! Besides, the food's always fabulous here, even though I do say it myself—' She had been hovering near the finds table and now peered into Josie's lunch-box with interest. The castle kitchens provided Josie with a mini-feast to go each day, and she could never finish it all.

'Have some,' she told her friend, who didn't need to be asked twice.

'You can't possibly miss one of Dario's parties!' Antonia insisted, choosing some mini-calzone.

'I shouldn't think I'm invited. I haven't heard anything about it.'

'Josie, you're a friend of the family—just walk in!'

'I don't think so,' Josie said uncomfortably. 'That's not how parties work where I come from. In any case, I'll have more than enough to do, cataloguing all the finds from this little spot.

Work and an early night. You know that's what I'm here for, after all.'

   *...Although now I can't help wishing that Dario himself might come and sweep me away from all this,* she thought wistfully.

# CHAPTER SIX

ANTONIA promised to return and help Josie catalogue her finds, once she had put Fabio down for an afternoon nap. When a brand new four-by-four painted with the di Sirena logo came rolling along the drove road towards her excavation, Josie assumed Antonia had managed to get away at last, but it wasn't her friend who had come to find her. When the vehicle stopped, a member of the castle staff climbed out of the driving seat. The man carried a large transparent box, so Josie could see before he handed it to her that it was full of artist's materials.

'Oh, wow!' she said in delight. 'Thank Count Dario very much for me. This is perfect!' she called after the driver as he got back into his vehicle and drove away.

Opening the container, she breathed in the

wonderful, very particular aroma of brand new pencils, brushes and paper. Her fingers itched to start work.

*Why not?* she thought, filled with devilment at the idea of trying something that wasn't on her written list of things to do. There was no one to see. Dario himself had encouraged it, *and if he thinks I'm good enough...* she thought, unable to remember anyone praising her artwork before. That made her feel good in a way that was somehow more satisfying, more *personal* than praise for her academic work had ever been. When she spotted a formal white envelope tucked in between a sketchbook and a watercolour pan, she began to feel really special.

Her heart beating faster by the second, Josie picked up the letter. She could hardly wait to rip it open and find out what it said, but the envelope alone was unique. It was faintly watermarked with the di Sirena mermaids, and addressed in fountain pen with bold copperplate handwriting. That was another reason to stop and stare.

*Dr J. L. Street,* she read.

She turned the letter over to find a red blob of glisteningly official sealing wax. It had been impressed with the magnificent crest of the di Sirena family. She let out her breath in a whistle. It was almost as grand as a medieval manuscript! Easing it open, she found that the envelope was lined with fine grey tissue paper. It contained a single sheet of deckle-edged notepaper folded neatly around a large, thick white card. Looking at the letter first, she found a couple of exquisitely written lines:

*Dear Josie, here are a few things I selected for you at random. If you need anything more, let me know.*

It was signed with the single word 'Dario', which flowed across the page like the faint but distinctive tang of his aftershave.

His note had enclosed an invitation like nothing she had ever seen in her life before:

*The pleasure of your company is requested at a grand charity ball on the 18th July, hosted by Count Dario di Sirena. Evening dress to be worn.*

She read from the stiff card, embellished with gold tracery, and, wide-eyed with astonishment, she shook her head in disbelief.

*This is amazing!* she thought. *Fancy getting an official invitation to something like that! I can't believe it...and my mum certainly never will... it almost makes me wish I had the nerve to go...*

She let out a long drawn-out moan of disappointment. The thought of seeing Dario formally dressed again was almost enough to make her accept the invitation, even though she was sure Antonia was behind it. She knew Dario must look truly magnificent in his natural surroundings of a glittering formal party, wearing a tuxedo and strolling around with a glass of champagne in his hand. It made him all the more alluring, and it made Josie certain that she had to turn down his invitation.

She was tongue-tied enough in his presence. His party would be filled with people she didn't know, and with whom she had nothing in common. That would be bad enough, but to feel like that while she was in Dario's company would be unbearable. He had all the social skills and charm, while she had none. Though Josie was honest enough to admit that wasn't the whole reason. If her heart had felt at risk from their kiss by the pool, what would happen when she was at a party, where Dario was in his element? It felt as though this invitation tempted her further away from the world she knew—from where it was safe.

Josie stared at the wonderful invitation for a long time. Then she slid it back into its envelope and tucked it away in her bag with real regret. There was nothing for it. She sat down at her table to write a polite refusal—but didn't even get as far as 'Dear Dario'. That was no way to reply to an invitation like this. She would have to do it face to face. Standing up, she took two steps towards the *castello*, then went and sat down again. It was hard enough looking Dario in the eyes, without having to resist the temptation to throw caution to the wind and go to the ball.

She picked up her phone, but it took a while before she could press the right keys in the right order. When one of Dario's staff answered instead of him, she almost laughed with relief.

'I'm just ringing to let Count Dario know that I'm not able to attend his party,' she said in a sparkling rush, then ran out of words. The PA merely thanked her politely, and put down the phone. Josie stared at her handset. Turning down Dario's invitation was bad enough. Having her refusal accepted as a matter of course was worse.

Dario frowned at the slip of paper he had been handed by his PA. Its message presented him with another novelty. As always seemed to happen these days, Josie was at the bottom of it. People had been known to crawl from their sick-beds to attend one of his parties, but she had looked perfectly fit and well when he last saw her. He smiled, lingering over that image of her lithe, toned body. It didn't seem right that she should deny herself the chance of an evening's entertainment. She ought to make the most of every opportunity the Castello Sirena could offer while she was here.

Picking up his phone, he got her number and rang her in person.

'Everyone else jumps at the chance of attending a Castello Sirena party,' he said without bothering to introduce himself.

'I'm sorry, Dario. Parties aren't really my thing.'

She sounded uncertain, and he wasn't so easily deterred. 'I know you said you weren't wild about the social life in Rimini, but this will be different.'

'No, it won't. Not unless your social circle has

magically shrunk away to nothing, or is composed solely of archaeologists.'

'*Dannazione!* Now why didn't *I* think of that before I had all those invitations sent out? I could have included the staff of the National Museum!' he drawled with lilting amusement. He added, 'Don't forget there will be at least one other archaeologist there—Antonia.'

'And I'm sure she'll love the chance to play the part of hostess again—I don't want to get in her way. I'm sorry, Dario, but I won't be there. Better luck next time.'

'And would you really be more likely to attend "next time"?'

'Er…' she hesitated, but knew lying was impossible; Dario was bound to know she wasn't telling the truth '…probably not, no.'

'Is that your final decision?'

'I'm afraid so. It was really kind of you to invite me, Dario. I'd better leave the partying to those who can appreciate it,' she said, unable to suppress the note of wistfulness in her words.

'OK…' he said, then went silent.

'Are you still there?' she said after a pause.

'I was waiting for you to change your mind.'

She had to laugh at that. 'Well, I'll give you ten out of ten for persistence, but it's not going to happen, Dario!'

'Fine,' he said, and then he was gone.

In the years since Arietta's death, Dario had re-played their final, fatal row a million times in his mind. He had vowed long ago that he would never make the same mistakes again and, so far, he hadn't. If a woman decided to go her own way, that was fine by him. If she wanted to leave, he would open the door, thank her for her time and show her out.

*But Josie actually sounded sorry that she couldn't come,* he thought. Letting out a curse, he jumped up and decided he needed a distraction.

'I'm going out for a ride,' he called out to any-one who could hear, uncharacteristically leaving his staff to worry about his appointments for the rest of the day.

Heading straight for Ferrari's stable, he pulled his saddle off its tree but, after a moment's consideration, dropped it back down again. Vaulting onto the stallion's broad back, he rode out of the stable yard and into the estate. His mood was so black, it transmitted itself straight to his horse. Pointing him in the direction of the far hills, Dario gave Ferrari his head. He was so deep in thought it was only as he reined in the horse after their pipe-opener that he realised how far their gallop had taken them. The silvery streak in the far distance was the drove road. He was heading towards the old olive press—and Josie's dig.

Things had got right out of control. Now he couldn't even take an innocent ride in the country without winding up on her doorstep.

*Why can't I take what she says at face value?* he thought irritably. *Why can't I get her out of my mind?*

*Dr Josie Street's problem is that she can't see further than her next intellectual puzzle,* Dario decided. Her life was so lacking in fun, she hardly knew what the word meant. She not only refused to go to his party, she would rather use a telephone to tell him, rather than come out with it face to face. There must be something wrong, something lurking behind her stubborn single-mindedness. Grimly determined to find out what it was, he came to a decision. Josie would learn to relax and enjoy her stay at the *castello* if he had to stand over her and supervise her every moment.

*And her every movement,* he thought, suddenly struck by a vision of Josie in that wet white T-shirt.

Coming back to reality, he had two choices. He could let well alone, turn right and head straight back to his studio. There, he could take out his frustrations on a new canvas.

Or he could turn left and give Dr Josie Street an experience she would never forget.

The result was a foregone conclusion. Dario pulled out his mobile and made one short, succinct phone call to Antonia. Then he turned Ferrari's head in the direction of the old olive press and rode out like the last in a long line of conquering heroes.

At first, the sound was only the smallest disturbance in the summer day. The continuous scratchy songs of grasshoppers under the hot Tuscan sun absorbed the unusual sound until it was close enough to resolve itself into the regular rhythm of a walking horse.

Josie dropped her trowel. Every nerve in her body went on high alert. When the jingle of harness joined the steady reverberation of hoof beats, she got out of her trench. The sun reflected off the glittering white dust of the drove road, making her raise one arm to shade her eyes against the glare. There was nothing to see—yet. The approaching horseman was hidden by a dip in the track, but Josie didn't need to see him to know who it was. Something deep within her soul told her it was Dario, and he was coming for her.

Time stood still for her the second she saw that dark tousled head, contrasting so vividly with his golden skin and dazzling white shirt. It was revealed with tantalising slowness as he made his way relentlessly towards her. Flashes of painful brilliance seared her retinas as his horse's bridle glinted in the sunlight. She hardly noticed. When he drew so close she could smell the rich mixture of saddle soap and leather, she wondered if the power of speech had deserted her completely. Now was the time to find out.

'Dario.'

His name sizzled on her lips as it hit the dry air.

'Josie.'

Thickened by the heat, his accent made her name sound more foreign and exotic than ever.

'Are you here because I turned down your invitation?'

He straightened his back, becoming every inch the dignified aristocrat. 'No. That was your decision. This has nothing to do with the invitation, but it does have everything to do with you, Josie.'

The chill in his voice sent her backing into the canopy pole. She was like the figurehead of a ship, clutching at the last point of stability as her universe rolled and bucked around her.

'I've come to take you home with me, Josie.'

She moistened her dry lips with the tip of her tongue, very slowly.

'What? *Why?*' Her voice was barely a whisper, but his explanation was strong and sure.

'Antonia needs your help,' he announced.

Primed for him to admit that he wanted her, Josie deflated with sudden, sharp disappointment. She felt her fingers release their grip on the aluminium pole. Her hands fell to her sides and she walked forward onto the drove road. When Dario didn't automatically move his horse to fall in step beside her, she stopped and looked back at him quizzically.

'I came to give you a lift.'

He ran his hand down Ferrari's mane to make the point that they were a team, and for the moment Josie was the odd one out.

'You're not serious?'

The thought of being carried home was more frightening than Josie wanted to let on. Her gaze ran over the sleek sides of the horse but fell short of the powerful, brooding form of its rider. Her silence told Dario more than she wanted to put into words.

'Don't tell me you can neither swim nor ride?' He was incredulous.

'There isn't much call for either, down in a trench.'

'That doesn't matter. There's nothing to it. And, in any case, I shall be the one doing the riding—all you have to do is put your arms around my waist.'

Josie's gaze rose almost shyly to include Dario as well as Ferrari.

'So I'd be sitting behind you?' she said slowly.

'Yes.'

'Oh...' she said eventually. Her voice was little more than a whisper, but the heat of excitement powering through her veins was more fierce than the summer sun. Dario was wrong. If he had ridden up and swept her into his arms without a word she wouldn't have been able to utter a single complaint. She would have been stunned into silence, and an all too willing and dangerous surrender.

Dario's immense self-confidence transmitted itself to Ferrari, who paced obediently over to the shade of an ancient, almost horizontal olive tree growing at the wayside. Horse and rider were infused with the arrogant pride of centuries, and all Josie could do was obey.

'The trunk of this tree slopes gently enough to make a perfect mounting block.'

Josie looked at it speculatively. As there was

no alternative, she hopped up onto the lowest point of the sun-warmed tree. While she tentatively edged her way along its trunk, Dario backed his horse in close.

Josie was scared, but couldn't bear to say so. She looked at Dario, and he saw the fear in her eyes.

'Don't think—put your hands on my shoulders and just do it.'

She thought back to the pool, and remembered that moment of exhilaration just after she fell into the water. Dario had caught her up and saved her from drowning, only to flood her with a bewitching torrent of feelings that had tortured her from that moment on.

*And it's starting all over again,* she realised as the heat of his gaze raked over her body.

Sitting astride his horse, he looked and sounded supremely confident. There was no hint of threat about him, merely the majesty of a man on his own land.

*He must be right. This will be perfectly OK,* she persuaded herself.

Taking her courage in both hands, she did as Dario told her and found herself sitting behind him, astride Ferrari. She was so scared her lungs almost stopped working. All she could get were little panting breaths of the hot dry air.

'Relax, Josie! This is the perfect way to travel.' Dario's voice was a purr of reassurance, but she was far too tense to appreciate it.

'Only when you're used to it,' she said in a thin, strained voice. It sounded at least an octave higher than normal.

'You will feel safer if you put your arms around my waist rather than gripping my shoulders.'

'Will I?' The doubt in her voice was so obvious she felt his laughter rumble up from beneath his ribs before she heard it.

'Try it.'

Josie had to summon up a lot more nerve before she could loosen her hands, one at a time, to take a terrifyingly light grip around his ribcage.

'I won't break.' He chuckled, and she felt the movement dance though his whole body.

'Why is your horse called Ferrari?' She looked down with apprehension. The ground seemed a horribly long way away.

There was a pause. 'Because he is very fast, and dangerous in the wrong hands,' Dario said in a voice rich with meaning.

Josie made a conscious effort to keep her hands loose on Dario's sides, but it was almost impossible. The warmth of him begged to be experienced skin to skin, without the bother of fear, clothes or anything else.

'Do you feel safe?'

'Compared with what?' she asked in a small, quavering voice. The horse's back felt very warm and tense beneath her. 'Does it get any worse than this?'

'I won't let it. Loosen up, Josie. I'll keep you safe.'

Dario's deep brown voice persuaded her to try to relax. His confidence was infectious.

Gradually she felt it loosen her limbs, and so did Ferrari. The surface she was sitting on became mobile in several different directions at once as Dario directed his horse back onto the drove road.

'How does that feel? Better?'

'Ask me after I've got off at the other end. It's probably one of those experiences that's better viewed in hindsight,' she croaked.

'A simple OK would do. Or *suffice,* if you like, Dr Street.'

'Now you're laughing at me again,' she accused.

'No...never. I'm trying to get you to relax, and maybe distract you a little. You'll enjoy the experience much more if you do. Listen to that—' He pointed to one of the resident skylarks swinging up towards the heavens. 'You'd never hear that from inside a car.'

'No, but I can enjoy the same sounds while I'm safely down in my trench.'

'Only with the little bit of your brain that isn't

wrapped up in your work. Where is your sense of adventure, Josie? This way you get to enjoy everything my home has to offer, so much more intimately.' He paused, and she felt his ribcage expand as he drew in a long breath. 'Mind you, I normally race around at top speed myself, travelling between appointments or chasing deadlines. Taking it this slowly is making me appreciate it more, too.'

'Don't you already know every inch of this estate? You and Antonia have both told me how you used to spend most of your time out here when you were children.'

'Yes, because it was safer than staying inside the castle,' Dario said quietly. 'If our parents were in residence, their fighting could easily spill over onto us. If they were away, on the yacht or at the ski lodge, say, Antonia and I had to run the gauntlet of the staff they'd bussed in to keep us clean and fed. That was always a bit of a lottery. The good ones left when they got fed up with living in chaos, and the bad ones got fired—eventually. We were left to run riot, roaming the hills when it was dry and dodging from house to house around the estate when the weather was bad. They say it takes a whole village to raise a child. That was certainly true in our case.'

Dario stopped suddenly, and Josie realised he'd said more than he'd meant to. In spite of desperately wanting to know more, she managed to act as if he'd simply carried on with small talk and, keeping a firm grip around his waist, looked out across the undulating countryside as he changed the subject and pointed out some of his old haunts.

'I've been invited into quite a few of those places already,' she told him. 'Everyone around here is really friendly. They always stop and chat.'

He laughed. 'I thought you hated being interrupted when you were working?'

'Yes…but there's something about this place that makes me want to learn more about the people living here today, rather than being buried in the past all the time.'

'That's good.' In a spontaneous movement, Dario dropped one hand and reached back. He touched her thigh, and patted it briefly. It was only a tiny movement, but it sent powerful messages surging through her body. With a sigh she felt herself submit to the waves of warmth travelling from his body to hers. Gradually she softened towards the experience. As she relaxed against him, her arms closed in around the reassuring solidity of his body. Before she knew what was happening, her cheek brushed his shoulder. It was just for a moment, but long enough to appreciate the clean soap and cologne fragrance of him.

She drew in a long, lingering breath of it. 'This is wonderful…' she murmured.

'Are you enjoying it, Josie?'

As always, his beautiful voice filled her name with colours she had never noticed before.

'I am. This is lovely.'

'Good. That's exactly as it should be. After all your hard work, you deserve a little treat or two. Some time off, and a few hours of indulgence.'

Josie thought about the party. She had so wanted to say yes to that invitation, she wished he would ask her again. Now she felt so safe in his presence, she would have been tempted to accept—but Dario was lost in thought. For some time, the only sounds were the skylarks, the jingle of harness and the regular dull thud of Ferrari's hooves on the dusty white track.

'You're right. I'm a lucky man. This place is wonderful,' he said at length.

# CHAPTER SEVEN

JOSIE was in heaven. Once she got used to the gentle rhythm of Ferrari's gait, she could think of nothing but the sensation of having her arms around Dario's waist. His body was so warm and vital. She could feel the play of his muscles as they moved beneath the thin white fabric of his shirt. It brought back all the bittersweet memories of their picnic in the wood, her fear…and his kisses… She closed her eyes. With each measured step they took, her breasts nudged tantalisingly against Dario's back. That made the growing fire inside her burn even brighter.

'You can lean against me all you like,' he said softly. 'If it will make you feel better.'

After a moment's hesitation, she did. It was hypnotically wonderful. Only the change in sound of Ferrari's hooves as they moved from the drove road to the gravel outside the stable yard persuaded her to open her eyes again and sit up straight.

'Wait. I'll lift you down,' Dario told her as a stable lad ran to take Ferrari's reins.

Wide awake now, Josie fizzed with excitement. Dropping lightly to the ground, Dario reached up and put his hands around her waist to lift her from the horse's back. When her feet touched the gravel she discovered exactly how much the experience had taken from her.

'My legs have gone to jelly!' she whispered, frantically grabbing at him. He put his arms around her to steady her and a shockwave pulsed through her body. Suddenly she was greedy for his touch and didn't want him to let her go.

'That's natural. And I'm in no hurry to go anywhere.'

'B…but you've always got another appointment somewhere or other…'

'That can wait for a few moments. I would never abandon you out here with jelly legs.'

Josie looked at him and it was well worth it. He was smiling.

*He's going to ask me about the party again and there's no way I can refuse!* she thought, breathless with panic and anticipation. *There's no way I can refuse him anything!*

But she had misjudged him.

A moment later, his fingers closed on her upper arms and he gently pushed her away. In that instant she felt the electric charge flowing through her body falter and fail as he broke the circuit.

'Goodbye, Josie,' he said in a husky voice.

And then he was gone.


All Josie's fantasies about being able to attend Dario's party shattered like a Ming vase. She tried to convince herself it didn't matter, but it did. Putting on a brave face, she walked into the castle to meet Antonia, although thoughts of what might have been were a permanent loop of regret running through her mind. *Couldn't she have said yes? Been brave, just for once? What was she going to do with her carefully protected heart anyway—keep it in a museum?*

'Now Fabio's asleep we can hit the town,' Antonia said confidently as she skipped downstairs from the nursery. 'What are you going to wear tomorrow night?'

'I'm not going.'

'Oh…still not? Why not?'

'I've got too much to do. You know how it is,' Josie said with a nonchalance that fooled neither of them.

'Well, *you* might be able to pass up the chance of a night of glamour and romance tomorrow, Jo, but that doesn't mean *I* have to. I want you to come and help me choose a dress for the party, and we can talk about your project at the old olive press while we do it. I told you there was plenty to discover here, didn't I?'

'You did—and you were absolutely right.' Josie wasn't just thinking of archaeology. She gazed through the open *castello* door at the sun-drenched forecourt outside. Dario would have to cross it on his way to or from the stables and garage complex, but the forecourt stayed deserted.

Despite the bright day, it felt as though her life had lost some of its sparkle. 'I'd love to come with you,' she said brightly, trying to summon up some genuine enthusiasm.

'Good. The chauffeur will have the limo here in a couple of minutes,' her friend said, grinning.

Shopping with Antonia on her home ground was a new experience for Josie. It couldn't have been more different from her everyday life back in England. Instead of dragging around crowded chain stores getting hotter and more frustrated by the second, this was an expedition into another world.

An air-conditioned di Sirena limousine swept them almost silently to Florence. They were dropped off within sauntering distance of the designer quarter. The streets were shady, with chic little cafés every few yards for the tired of spending. Before they could get too hot, Antonia paused outside her favourite designer's showroom. To Josie's amazement, they didn't even need to open the door for themselves. An assistant threw it back on its hinges at the mere sight of Antonia. They were greeted like royalty, and ushered into cool splendour. Josie decided this must have been what it was like to be shown into an ancient Roman temple, only this building was on a *much* more opulent scale. She stopped and stared, completely overawed by all the gold leaf and pink marble columns until Antonia took her in hand.

'Come and meet Madame, Jo. She makes all my clothes when I'm at home.'

Madame was a tiny Parisian in towering black stilettos, a chic little black dress and jet-black hair scraped back into a neat bun. She was the consummate European, flourishing her scarlet nails like a matador's cape to hypnotise and tempt. When they were formally introduced, Josie was so starstruck she almost bowed.

'Oh, lighten up, Jo!' Antonia laughed. 'The staff are here to serve *us*, not the other way around. Take a seat, dunk your biscotti, do whatever you want. They won't care!'

Cautiously, Josie let herself be shown to a seat. When Antonia ordered a latte, she did exactly the same, although she would rather have had a cup of tea. Then her friend was shown the finished dresses she had previously ordered from Madame's autumn collection, together with samples of a dozen new designs in a rainbow of colours. Once she knew she was safely out of the spotlight, Josie began to relax. Soon she was lounging in her comfortable armchair and offering her opinion to Antonia as confidently as Madame.

Then one of the covey of assistants emerged from a room at the back of the salon carrying a single dress reverently in her hands. It was a fluid length of shimmering silk in the most beautiful shade of green Josie had ever seen. She was vaguely aware of Antonia standing up for a closer look, but nothing could distract her from that stunning vision.

'You've got to try that on, Toni,' she said with longing. 'With your dark colouring, it would make you look really exotic.'

'You think?' Antonia took the ravishing cock-tail dress from the assistant, turning its hanger so that light danced over its discreet detail of gold threads. 'I don't know…bias cut is awfully unforgiving to a tummy like mine.' She chewed the inside of her cheek, then appeared to have a sudden inspiration.

'Tell you what, Jo—why don't *you* try it on? It would be a brilliant match for your eyes.'

'I don't know…' she said slowly, although deep down she did. They all did. There was no way any woman alive could have refused such an offer.

'Oh, come on—it'll look gorgeous!' Antonia smiled. 'You know you want to…'

Josie laughed in spite of herself, and gave in. 'All right,' she decided, struggling out of the depths of her comfy armchair before she could change her mind. 'I'll do it!'

Swishing the dress from Antonia's hands, she strode off to where an assistant was waiting to help her change. The changing room was nothing like the tiny curtained cubicles she was used to. It was larger than her flat back in England, and the surroundings made taking her clothes off in front of a complete stranger almost feel natural.

*Almost, but not quite!* she thought, blushing.

Unable to look at her reflection while she stripped, she concentrated on the lacy wisps of sweet-pea-coloured lingerie draped artistically around the room. Seeing all those lovely things made her ache to attend the party. For once in her life she would have given anything to dress up and strut her stuff, to show gorgeous Dario a completely different side of her. If only the single decent dress she had brought to Italy wasn't so old and enormous. She had bought it for her engagement party, but Andy's subsequent betrayal and her retreat into overwork had seen the weight fall off her. She had thought it would be good enough to wear for private dinners at the *castello*, but that was before she'd actually met Dario. Nothing would have persuaded her to wear it now.

Suddenly shy at dressing up in the lovely green silk dress, she pulled it on hurriedly, half afraid to look. The assistant's gasp horrified her.

'Oh, no—don't say I've wrecked it?'

Hideous scenes of split seams or gashed silk filled her mind as she glanced at the mirrored wall beside her.

One glimpse and she stopped, awestruck. The dress was perfect.

*And so am I!* she thought before modesty caught up with her. She turned pink at the thought.

The assistant was first to come to her senses. She flung open the changing room door and stood back, motioning for Josie to walk out into the showroom.

The collective intake of breath from Antonia, Madame and all her assistants was worth every second of self-doubt Josie had ever suffered in her life. She instantly felt taller, more self-confident and...

'*Wow*, Josie!' Antonia breathed reverently. 'You're *beautiful*!'

'Yes,' she said shakily, managing to agree with a compliment for the first time in her life. It gave her a little shiver of shock. She was amazed to find that was another sensation she liked.

'What do you think they'd say if I walked into the university Christmas ball wearing this, Toni?'

'They wouldn't say anything,' her friend sighed. 'They wouldn't be able to.'

Madame was not amused. 'That dress might have been made with you in mind. You simply must have it, Dr Street.'

With those words, Josie stopped looking de-lighted and started looking worried. She discreetly mouthed a desperate question across at her friend. *'How much is it?'*

'Oh, you don't need to worry about that,' Antonia said airily.

'But I do!' Josie said aloud.

'Think of it as a birthday present. Happy birthday,' Antonia said.

'But it's not my birthday.'

Antonia smiled more enigmatically than the Mona Lisa. 'I know,' she said mysteriously.

Although she couldn't wait to get back to the *castello* to try on her new dress again, Josie got her generous friend to take her from the salon to a chain store, where she felt happier and could spend her own money. Now she was discovering how much fun it was to be spontaneous, there was no stopping her.

As she was indulging herself with satin and lace, Dario's words about wanting to know when she felt like doing something scarily spontaneous came back to her with a guilty rush of excitement.

*I wonder exactly how spontaneous I can be?* she thought to herself with a sudden burst of bravado. *I might surprise you yet, Count Dario di Sirena!*

'I could gatecrash…' she said, not realising that she had said it out loud.

'Do what?' Antonia replied absently, her attention on some ankle bracelets.

Josie blushed, but then went for broke. 'The party. Antonia, can I come to the party after all?'

Antonia looked around at Josie with a broad smile. 'Yes! I thought you'd never ask!' she said, throwing her arms around her friend.

'But I've already refused Dario's invitation, not once, but twice!' Josie frowned.

'He won't mind, but if you're going to worry you can come as my guest. Everyone's allowed a "plus one", so tell yourself you're mine,' Antonia said, as quick as a flash.

'You have an answer for everything.' Josie shook her head in awe.

Antonia smiled a wicked smile. 'Of course. It's called native cunning.'

Dario was in his studio, trying to plan a new painting. He couldn't settle to anything and had tried to find some way of filling the time while Antonia and Josie were in Florence. First, he'd gone out on Ferrari again. That had been unsettling. Every step of the way recalled Josie's arms around his waist, her body pressed tight against his. Before he'd known it, he had accidentally reached the old olive press where her boxes of finds and tools stood neatly packed away beneath the awning that protected her work. It was his own land and he had visited the place a hundred times over the years, but it felt like an intrusion to be there alone today. He'd seen the box he had sent her and, looking more closely, noticed she had already unpacked a sketchbook and made a start.

Unused to feeling uncomfortable on his home ground, Dario had turned Ferrari's head away from the place so full of Josie's presence. He thought it would be cooler to ride up through the trees. Instead, his temperature rose as he drew closer to the place in that woodland glade where he had kissed her. Not for the first time, her spirit disrupted his plans.

*I've only known her a few days, and yet she's on my mind all the time. I can taste the sweetness of her lips and feel the warmth of her body, even when she's miles away. What's the matter with me?* he thought restlessly. He couldn't concentrate on his work. He decided to try to replace all his thoughts of her with something else, and fast.

That was when he had abandoned the wide expanse of his estate for the contained luxury of his studio. Hoping to lose himself in his art, Dario soon found another of his usually perfect cures wasn't up to the task. In a complete change of direction, he started to paint a portrait. Things went wrong from the beginning. The subject of his portrait was supposed to be Arietta. To Dario's irritation, his preliminary sketches kept turning into someone else entirely—and that 'someone' looked uncannily like Dr Josephine Street.

When a flash of sunlight danced around the room, he was glad of the distraction. Then he saw it was reflecting off a sleek black car as it slid along the lime avenue towards the front door.

*It's Josie!* He threw down his stick of charcoal, then snatched it up again.

*No. It's Antonia. And...her friend,* he corrected himself carefully, resisting the temptation to go out and welcome them home.

Josie hurried straight up to her own suite. The moment she was safely inside, she started unpacking all the carrier bags she had brought back from Florence. Reverently, she put the beautiful dress Antonia had bought her on one of the padded hangers. Then she carried it up to the top floor of her suite and hung it up in the room Dario had called the solar. That way, she could see it while she worked. At least, that was the theory. Once the dress was displayed in sun-lit glory, it was all Josie could do to tear her-self away and unpack everything else she had bought. Antonia had exploited her temporary brainstorm by suggesting another indulgence, which had prompted a real spending spree.

*Now you're coming to the party tomorrow night, Jo, we can have some real fun. I've ar-ranged for a masseuse and my usual team of beauticians to visit the castle. You and I can make a real day of it.*

From that moment on, Josie's work had to take a back seat, although, happily, in her attempts to drive Dario from her mind, she was far ahead with her research. She spent far more time ad-miring her new dress from every angle and counting down the minutes until her makeover. Whenever she thought about the party, she felt sick with nerves and excited at the same time. She took the tops off all the bottles of gel and bubbles and oils she had bought for the occasion and inhaled until she was high on a cocktail of jasmine and adrenalin.

When she finished what passed for work that day, she took the green silk down into her bedroom so she could carry on admiring it. When a maid came in to turn down her bed, Josie didn't have to ask if she liked the dress.

'You'll be the centre of attention at tomorrow night's party, *signorina*!' the girl whispered with awe.

Josie couldn't answer. All her worries about the celebrity guest list were coming back in force. She thought of the evening ahead and privately planned to spend the whole evening hiding behind a pillar if necessary, nice and close to the buffet.

Next day, Josie's work rate plummeted to zero but she hardly cared. Her worries about it were reduced to a tiny cloud hovering on the extreme edge of a much larger storm. Happily, the make-over took up nearly all her time, and it was heav-enly. Every moment brought her closer to the party, the dress…and Dario. That thought made her so nervous she could barely touch the little party savouries that Antonia kept ordering from the kitchens.

After a long soak in scented water right up to her neck, Josie had an aromatherapy massage with rose oil. While she was trapped beneath a hairdresser's skilful fingers and with a mani-curist at work on each hand, Antonia seized her moment.

'I'm so pleased you decided to come to the party, Jo. You never know. It might be an intro-duction to that tall, dark, handsome man who'll sweep you off your feet.'

Josie could only think of one person who fitted that description: Dario. She had been thinking about nobody else, and was suddenly afraid she might give herself away. She tried to distract Antonia with a careless laugh.

'Hah! The last time that happened, my heart got kicked down the road like a tin can,' she said, trying to sound as though it didn't matter.

'Andy Dutton was neither tall, nor dark, nor handsome,' Antonia huffed.

Josie recoiled from the memory of the biggest romantic disaster of her life. 'That's why I've come to a decision. I've decided it's time to put that whole horrible business behind me and move on,' Josie announced bravely, and immediately felt better for saying it. Once she had put her feelings into words, things suddenly felt so much clearer in her mind. 'I'm only sorry I couldn't have realised it sooner,' she sighed.

'So you've finally come around to my way of thinking? That it's time to forget him?' Antonia grinned, delighted.

'Yes—and no. I may have recovered from getting my feelings burned by Andy, but it's made me determined never to get so close to that particular kind of fire again,' she said, but as she spoke, the memory of Dario's kisses flooded through her. How could she say such things, yet still feel like this? Thoughts of his hard, hot body beneath her hands filled her with a longing that all the massage oils in the world could never relieve—and the sensation was spectacular.

'Fine—so tonight you're not looking for trouble, you're just there to enjoy yourself,' Antonia said airily. 'What can possibly go wrong with that?'

'I'm not looking for anything,' Josie announced, trying hard to convince herself that it was true.

Her mind was too full of Dario for safety. Dealing with that would be more than enough for her to handle.

As the day went on, time slowed down to a snail's pace. First, Josie's hair was piled up like a Roman princess. Then, when her fingers and toes had been thoroughly pampered, her nails were painted the colour of mother-of-pearl, making them shimmer with her slightest movement. Then she got the chance to choose some diamond earrings from Antonia's collection of jewellery, and a pair of equally sparkly stilettos from her friend's huge collection of shoes. After that, time crawled by until there was barely half an hour to go before the party. Then Antonia started fluttering around her like a demented butterfly.

'I don't know how you can stay so calm, Jo!'

'I do all my panicking inside. Inside, I'm running about like a mad thing!' she added with a thrill of excitement, checking her watch for the fifth time. They stood together in Josie's drawing room, while Antonia fussed around her and they both waited for the staff to announce that the guests were arriving.

Finally, Antonia stood back to admire her handiwork. Josie couldn't resist glancing at herself in the full-length mirror the staff had set up for the occasion. It was incredible. Antonia was right—she was almost unrecognisable. A smile was the only thing she needed to make the picture absolutely perfect. Blushing with an unusual rush of pride, she looked away from her reflection quickly.

'Not even Dario would know it's you.' Antonia giggled as they got the call from the staff and went downstairs through the cool corridors of the great castle.

'Here's hoping,' Josie said as her heart began to accelerate. After everything she had told Dario about being determined not to come to his party, here she was. All it had taken was this beautiful dress, and the need to prove to him that she *could* enjoy herself when she wanted. Despite her nerves, she felt as if she were living in a fairy tale. She put a hand to her forehead. Was she delirious? Would she wake up to find she had been dreaming?

Antonia gently led her towards the great marble staircase. The sound of restrained small talk rose from the crowd of guests down in the foyer, each receiving their first glass of champagne.

*If I could lose myself in this mob, maybe I would feel less like a human sacrifice,* she thought, trying to feel relieved. As she came downstairs, her embarrassment level rose as a wave of silence spread through the crowd below. In the seconds before they remembered their manners and greeted their hostess, Josie felt the eyes of every person in the place trained on her. She and Antonia joined the straggle of other people heading away through the portrait gallery towards the castle's grand banqueting hall. They were all marvelling at the grand di Sirena ancestors, but Josie's attention was turned in a quite different direction. The portrait gallery ran around three sides of a glazed quadrangle which was open to the skies. There, the leaves of a big old apricot tree stirred in the sultry dusk.

She nudged Antonia. 'I think I might have changed my mind about this—I wish I was out there rather than in here!' she whispered.

'Rubbish. You'll love it once the party's started. Look how you dithered about coming to work here in the first place. I don't hear you worrying about putting anyone to any trouble now!'

*No,* thought Josie. *That's because all my other worries have faded in comparison, from the moment I met Dario.*

She sighed and tried to look on the bright side. She looked around at the flash and dazzle of diamonds and military medals worn by all the other guests. Why would he even look at her? Getting on well with his sister hardly counted in stellar company like this. Suddenly, her reckless giggle returned.

*Dario felt pretty impressed with me when we kissed!* she thought, and blushed. What would all these people think if they knew what was going through her mind?

The double doors to the great banqueting hall were open wide, so it would have been easy to slip inside unnoticed. Josie looked around. People had been smiling appreciatively at her from the moment she'd appeared at the top of the stairs. Trying to sneak in wouldn't stop them doing that. She might as well make the most of her few moments in the spotlight. If nothing else, it would be good practice for the university's Christmas ball. Taking a deep breath, she pulled herself up straight and tall and strode bravely into the room.

The banqueting hall was already bright with people, but the first and only thing she saw was Dario. He was standing in front of a cold marble fireplace, talking to a languid blonde in scarlet satin.

As Josie entered, there was a lull in the conversation. Dario's gaze was already raking the room, but at the sudden silence it swooped over to her, then back to his slender companion. A split second later, he executed the perfect double take. Looking across at Josie again, he trapped her in his gaze. It killed his conversation stone dead, and Josie froze. All the polite, charming, witty things she'd planned to say to him fled from her mind. She was left staring at him across the room, speechless with amazement.

Dario looked every bit as wonderful as she had known he would, each night when she'd heard him drive away into town. He was resplendent in a formal black dinner jacket and trousers with a plain white shirt and black bow-tie. His crisp shirt accentuated the pale gold of his colouring and the dark allure of his eyes—and that was where she got the biggest reward of all. His gaze was totally absorbed by her. He smiled suddenly, in such a genuine gesture of pleasure that Josie was lost. In that moment all her worries about gatecrashing his party dissolved. The naked desire in his expression sent her senses spinning. Her own burning need for him made her want to stride forward, push her fingers through his unruly tousle of curls and kiss him again and again, no questions asked.

Instead, she blushed, dropped her gaze and shuffled uncertainly on the spot.

Dario abandoned his companion without a

backward glance and crossed the room in a few strides. Taking Josie's hand, he lifted it to his lips.

'Josie...tonight, you could tempt a saint,' he breathed.

Speechless, she raised her eyes as his kiss connected with her fingers. Dario's gaze pinned her to the spot. She relished the feel of his skin against hers, and the touch of his fingers as they curled around her palm. He held her in a grasp that was strong, yet cool. At any other time, or in the hands of any other man, Josie would have pulled away. This perfect man, on this special night, was different.

*I'm going to enjoy every moment of this party,* she told herself, staggered by the realisation.

She looked around nervously. An appreciative crowd was smiling at the little scene being acted out in front of them. By the time her eyes flicked back to Dario, he had resumed his usual suave, unflappable charm.

'Thank you for coming, Dr Street. I know how much you dislike gatherings like this, and I'm flattered you chose to make an exception for mine.' He smiled, then added a compliment that sent shivers of anticipation dancing up and down Josie's spine.

'I've never seen a more lovely woman. Or one so beautifully dressed,' he said simply. 'You are without doubt the most beautiful guest here this evening.'

# CHAPTER EIGHT

JOSIE opened her mouth to say something, but every sensible thought in her mind had evaporated. She closed it again, and tried another smile. Luckily, those muscles were still working, despite the effect Dario was having on the rest of her body. She could only hope her expression spoke for her.

*No one has ever called me beautiful before. I've always been just ordinary old Jo, or Dr Street,* she thought.

'Now, I shall introduce you to some of my charming friends. They will take good care of you for me while I am doing my duty as host.'

Dario drew her away from the throng and towards a stout, cheerful-looking couple. Despite their expensive designer clothes, they had open, weather-beaten faces and expressions that Josie took to instantly.

'This is Signor and Signora Bocca. They own a neighbouring estate and their son—Beniamino—went off to university very recently. Dr Street will be able to put your minds at rest about undergraduate life,' he told them, giving Josie a wicked wink.

The couple chuckled, shamefaced.

'He's gone to the USA on a scholarship, and Antonia told me you worked in Iowa for a while last summer, Josie. Maybe you could tell them all about it?' He smiled.

'It'll be my pleasure, Dario,' she said, and it was true. Dario squeezed her hand in parting, and it felt as though he knew exactly what she was thinking.

Despite his affable smile, Dario was uneasy. Something strange was going on inside his head, and his body wanted its own way, too. Once again, it was all down to Josie. He tried to think, but it was difficult to do that while keeping a buoyant conversation going with the lovely Tamara. Dario felt duty-bound to keep a discreet eye on Josie, now she was here. He knew enough of her shyness to realise that attending his party after all must have taken a lot of courage. He was impressed and relieved at the same time. Although he enjoyed socialising, for the first time in his life he had felt like getting his staff to cancel a party at the last moment. Now Josie had arrived, he could admit her rejection had weighed on his mind like a lead weight. The second she'd walked in, everything had changed. Simply seeing her made him ready to relax and enjoy himself.

After a few more minutes of idly seductive chit-chat with Tamara, he realised something still wasn't right. The thought of spiriting this long-legged lovely away from the party left him cold. Tamara might be clever and charming, but suddenly that was no longer enough for him.

She would be a meaningless conquest, and their conversation had lost all its attraction for him.

Tamara was twinkling as she tried to win back Dario's attention, but his gaze took every opportunity to escape. He tried dragging it back to her as she told him some long and complicated story about her PA having to courier lost documents from one side of the EU to the other. He attempted to smile at all the right moments, but his heart wasn't in it. Tamara had everything— except his attention. He wished he could see straight through her and out the other side.

The only thing that could hold his gaze was a knot of local businessmen and dignitaries over in the far corner of the room.

*It has come to something when a girl like Tamara has fewer attractions for me than a bunch of men I speak to every day,* he thought, trying to ignore the obvious fact that it wasn't them holding his attention captive. It was the bright shining star at the centre of their universe.

Dario put a hand up to his neck and felt the

muscles as tight as steel hawsers. He had hoped this party would help him to let off some steam, relax a little. Right now he was feeling more tense than he had done in years. What had changed? His guests were all enjoying themselves hugely—Josie included.

*What's wrong with that?* he rebuked himself. *That's what parties are for, for God's sake—so people can come out and forget themselves for a while!*

That day in the glade, he had teased Josie about being unable to enjoy herself. As he watched her tonight, nothing looked further from the truth. She was revelling in all the attention, but Dario knew he had one big advantage over the men surrounding her. So far, he was the only one in the place who had taken his interest in her any further. With a flash of relief, he finally realised what had been torturing him for so long.

*I want to keep it that way.*

Josie was special. Her particular brand of intelligence and charm—not to mention her breathtaking appearance tonight—promised delights far beyond anything Tamara and his other coterie of lovelies could offer him. All he had to do was cross the room to where she stood. The other men were bound to defer to him at once.

*Don't disrupt her moment in the sun, Dario!* he growled to himself. *She's enjoying herself.*

He took a deep breath and tried to act on his own advice. Then he realised Tamara was reaching out to worm her long slender arms around his waist like overcooked vermicelli.

Dodging neatly out of her reach, he made some noises of regret and moved Tamara by the hand towards a gaggle of women discussing interior design with Antonia. Kissing her freshly powdered cheek as consolation, he abandoned her and began to work his way around the room.

Dario purposely set off to charm the guests furthest away from where Josie was holding court. It was a carefully calculated move. He was always scrupulous about observing the social niceties. As the host, he had a duty to all his guests, not just to his favourite ones. But, all the time, every fibre of his being ached for Josie, her company, her laughter, her...*everything*. Finally, after the longest hour of his life, hers was the last little clique on his circuit. With one hand, he lifted a glass of champagne from a nearby tray, then stuck the other into his trouser pocket and sauntered casually to the edge of her group.

'Josie...'

He spoke, and she smiled.

Dario took that as his cue to advance and stand beside her. Instead of lifting her fingers to his lips as he had done the first time they'd met, on impulse, his hand went straight to her waist as he kissed her lightly on the cheek. She didn't flinch from either gesture, he noticed with a delicious kick of pleasure.

'How are you enjoying the party?'

'I didn't think you'd recognise me,' she said apprehensively.

'I would know you anywhere,' he said, and it was true. She was so lovely, he couldn't bear to leave her alone for a moment. No one knew more than he did how every single second in the company of a beautiful woman should be cherished. One wrong word, one thoughtless gesture and happiness could be snatched away for ever. Nothing could have persuaded him to risk going through the pain he'd endured in losing Arietta—but he wasn't prepared to see Josie fall prey to one of his guests. The idea of a treasure like her in the clutches of another man was unthinkable.

'I really am so glad you felt able to come,' he said before she had time to think. His fingers were still resting just below her ribcage. When she didn't automatically pull away, he let them linger, but only fractionally longer than good manners should have allowed. However, Josie seemed uneasy and her eyes flicked away, in the direction of another group of guests. He waited, puzzled. She did it again. Then he realised she was looking at the woman he had abandoned when he'd blazed a trail around the room to her.

'Oh, that's just Tamara,' Dario said casually, stepping back.

On the other side of the room, the blonde raised one hand and blew him a kiss.

'Hmm. It doesn't look as though she's saying, "Oh, that's just Dario," to those other people,' Josie said stiffly.

Dario felt a surge of purely male satisfaction. She was jealous—tonight she was as good as his.

'Would you like me to introduce you to her?' he said innocently. 'We've been friends—just friends—for years.' He smiled, and her lovely face lit up with a promise that was reflected all through her body. He saw her tension vanish. She took two languid steps towards him like a gentle breeze, and the effect was instantaneous. Dario forgot all about keeping control or seducing her slowly. All he wanted to do was take possession of her.

'I meant what I said, Josie. I'm really glad you decided to come after all,' he murmured.

'After you kept telling me that I should relax more? How could I do anything else?'

His dark eyes sparkled with amusement. 'You're the very last person I'd expect to find a party relaxing. I assumed you'd take up residence in my library tonight, as it's the least likely place to find other guests. Have you seen my library yet?'

'Yes. It was all very...*interesting*,' Josie said tactfully.

He smiled. 'That's a good answer. One of my forebears bought a lot of those books by the yard, back in the nineteenth century.'

She nodded. 'That explains the strange order they're in.'

'Not necessarily. My staff don't always bother to put things back in the proper place after I've read something.'

'You actually read those books?' she marvelled.

Dario took a sip of champagne. 'I'd invite you to come and look at them again with me sometime, but I know what your reaction to that would be.'

'You never know.'

'After our picnic the other day?'

'I've changed my usual clothes for this evening, and my appearance. How do you know I haven't changed in other ways?' she teased him back.

'Because a mermaid can never forsake the sea.'

Josie giggled, and lifted her glass to scrutinise its contents. 'This must be very good champagne. I'm not entirely sure I understood that!'

'In that stunning outfit, you would make the perfect mermaid.' His hand went to her hair, delicately lifting a strand back into place.

'Josie…in honour of this special occasion I should like to offer you a little memento.'

She was so carried away by the look of appreciation in his eyes that he might have been offering her the moon. Nodding wordlessly, she saw him signal to one of his staff. The man disappeared, only to hurry up to them a few seconds later, holding a spray of white cymbidiums, their throats flecked with pink and cream spots.

Dario took the flowers with a nod of thanks and smiled. 'The most beautiful flowers, for my most beautiful guest. May I?'

'Yes, please,' Josie breathed.

Dario took another step closer to her, so that his smart black shoes were toe to toe with the sparkly little stilettos she had borrowed from Antonia. Then he slid the fingers of one hand between her dress and the pale skin of her breast. Lifting the fine material away, he pinned the orchids safely to her shoulder.

'There,' he said, taking his time to remove his fingers. They trailed gracefully over her skin, making her delicate tan seem pale in contrast to his nut-brown fingers. She shivered at the delicious friction of their touch, but made no move to stop him or pull away, not even when she saw him take the opportunity to admire the swell of her breasts beneath the fabric of her dress and the delicate line of her throat.

His gaze moved back to her face and he smiled down at her. 'I also suspect that your adoring fans will soon block your way to the buffet. Let me act as your pilot.'

Without waiting for Josie's reply, he slid his arm lightly around her waist and swept her around the vast room with flair. Everyone turned to watch as they passed. They were all smiling and with satisfaction Dario saw that Josie was, too.

The buffet had been set up on a long row of polished tables in an anteroom. It was a feast for all the senses. Flower arrangements in the di Sirena colours of blue and gold, pyramids of tropical fruit and baskets of hand-made bread rolls in every shape and variety all gave off a wonderful fragrance. Light from the chande-liers dazzled over silver trays and crystal bowls of titbits. Dario knew the glorious sight and the polite murmur of conversation surrounding it would make both her work and England seem a very long way off for Josie—and that was exactly what he wanted.

Dismissing a footman who offered to help, he lifted a plate from the nearest stack of delicate china and handed it to her himself.

'You've barely touched your champagne. Shall I get you a soft drink instead?'

'No, this is wonderful.' Josie took a sip, but he could tell it was just for the look of the thing. Her attention was riveted on him.

*She is making real progress,* he thought, watching her expand beneath the warmth of his gaze like a beautiful butterfly emerging from a chrysalis. There was a glow of confidence about her tonight that she usually only wore while working. Dario had never given much thought to her hair before, but now he had to fight the urge to reach out and touch it all the time. Instead of being scraped back in a formidably efficient ponytail, it was arranged in a glorious confection which seemed spun from barley sugar. Her lovely dress left her arms and most of her shoulders bare, and he could see the tan line left by the short sleeves of the simple tops she usually wore. Wherever her skin had been exposed to the Tuscan sun, the past few days had toasted it to light gold. He found the contrast delicious. Her legs never normally saw the light of day when hidden by her working uniform of white T-shirt and overalls, and he looked down to see if they were pale, too. The room was warm and, as far as Dario was concerned, it was getting warmer by the second.

'I'm so sorry I messed you about over your invitation, Dario,' she murmured. 'I haven't enjoyed a party so much for…well, *ever*!'

Dario smiled away her apology. He liked the way her breath was coming in nervous little laughs tonight. The chandeliers high above threw dancing shadows as she moved, accentuating the tempting depths of her cleavage. The fine material of her dress showed him something else. The rise of her nipples was so blatantly obvious through the silk of her bodice, Dario could forgive her anything. And, now she was with him, he felt more relaxed than he could remember.

In contrast, Josie couldn't stand still. Once she had made up her mind to think only of enjoying herself, it was as if her body had woken up from a long hibernation. The nearness of Dario sent sparks fizzing up and down her spine. Although more guests were arriving at the buffet all the time, she was only aware of him and every movement he made—offering her first choice of all the delicious dishes on display, or half turning to talk to someone beside him. She felt almost too shy to look at him directly, but that hardly mattered. His slightest movement sent the delicate notes of his vanilla and spice after-shave wandering through the air between them. His fine, capable hands moved briefly into her line of vision now and again as he reached for something to pass to one of his guests. Polite and attentive, he kept every conversation light and easy. Josie was glad—she could hardly think of a thing to say. The sound of his voice was like deep water, tempting her to go closer than might be safe. And then…

And then, in the crush of people around the buffet table, they were jostled together. Josie felt his hand go to her bare shoulder, steadying her. Her head jerked around, but she found her automatic challenge calmed by one of Dario's special smiles. The feel of his body pressed against hers made Josie blush, and not in anger.

'I always assumed that life in a grand *castello* like this would be very prim and proper,' she managed to say, then gasped as he slyly glided his hand down over her back until it found a resting place at her waist. At the loss of his touch, it was all Josie could do to suppress a moan of disappointment.

Desire left her feeling light-headed. The room suddenly felt very hot. She rode this wave of warmth and waited to be engulfed by another embarrassing blush. Then she realised something else was happening to her body. Heat wasn't only travelling upwards. It was circling in a liquid coil of excitement, centred on a part of her body that had always been more trouble than it was worth in the past. Tonight, it made her feel spectacular. There was barely a whisper of a gap between her body and Dario's. Only the decency of their clothes stood between the subtle friction of his skin against hers. Josie's lips parted. She felt a little gasp escape. It wasn't loud enough for anyone else to hear, but Dario noticed. She smiled at him—a tentative look from beneath her eyelashes, but he understood. His bland expression dissolved and his eyes blazed with desire before he smiled, slowly.

'You sound hot, Josie,' he said in a low voice. 'When we've chosen our food, why don't we take it somewhere a little cooler?' ...*and more private*, was the assumption.

This was about much more than simply relaxing. Josie knew it would be so easy to say yes to Dario—but so dangerous. She could hardly wait to experience the luxury of his kisses again, although she knew that would be just the beginning. She could not expect a man like him to be satisfied with a single kiss—and, with a certainty that scared her, Josie knew she wanted more than that, too. Since Andy had abandoned her she had resisted every other attempt to sweet-talk her into bed, but tonight was different. Dario was unique.

'That would be good,' she said slowly.

He raised his eyebrows. 'Is that all?'

'For the moment.' She adjusted her corsage of orchids. 'You have all your other guests to satisfy first, don't forget.' The double meaning was deliberate, and both she and Dario knew it.

'I've spoken to everyone else already and they're mingling quite happily. So, as it's my special night, it's time I found something to satisfy *me*.' The blatant hunger in his eyes made her mouth go dry and her breath catch. Suddenly it was impossible to tear her eyes from his and for a long moment they simply stood, gazes locked, while the rest of the world seemed to melt away.

Josie felt as though she were falling down

Alice's rabbit hole, as though after tonight she'd emerge a whole new person. Feeling suddenly overwhelmed at what that might mean, she wrenched her eyes away and concentrated on the canapés, helping herself to a couple of tiny lobster crostini. She took a deep breath, determined to change the subject.

'This really is the most wonderful party, Dario.'

'I thought you weren't keen on parties,' he said slyly.

'True, yet I've never in my life been to something as opulent as this.'

'Then you're glad you came?'

'Definitely. It's the best party I've ever been to. Well, unless you count my birthdays!'

'Oh, so you do indulge yourself sometimes, then?'

She laughed. 'Not really. It's just something my mum has always done for me, every year for as long as I can remember. She makes a cake just big enough for the two of us, supposedly in secret, and we splash out on a takeaway—someone else does the cooking, and there's no washing-up. A bit like this—only about a thousand times smaller!' she joked.

'It must be wonderful to have someone think so much of you that they do that for you every year.'

'You'd swap all this for that?' She laughed.

'Yes. I would.'

She looked at him, incredulous, and noticed a trace of wistfulness in his expression.

'You're not telling me you've never been given a birthday party?'

'No, I never have.'

'Not even when you were tiny?'

He shook his head.

'Dario, that's awful!'

'It was the same for Antonia.' He shrugged off her concern.

'No wonder she used to love to party all night, every chance she got.'

He smiled wryly. 'I think it was certainly part of it. How did you cope, sharing a flat?'

'When I'd had enough, I used to go and stay at Andy's—when he was my fiancé. Obviously, that stopped when...' Josie paused in surprise. The normal dull stab of pain hadn't come when she'd mentioned Andy's name. Perhaps, on this glittering evening, with this beautiful man, she could leave the past behind. She remembered what Dario had said: *foolish man, not to see what he had.* Just for a moment, she felt it might have been true.

'Don't think of him now.' Dario reached out and brushed a strand of shining hair behind her ear.

'No! I want to tell you.'

Suddenly, she wanted Dario to know her sad little story, as though in saying it, she would be free.

'Andy didn't just cheat, you see. He'd been having an affair for a while, and it turned out quite a few members of the faculty had known all about it. I found out he had been putting it around that I was… That he wasn't getting…' She blushed and went silent.

'I'm sorry. I had no idea,' Dario said grimly.

'I'm still surprised Antonia hasn't told you all about this,' she said, looking at him acutely as she moved away from the table. Dario shadowed her closely.

'I may have practically raised my little sister single-handed, but that doesn't mean we discuss each other's friends.' He guided Josie away from the crowds.

She twitched a shoulder, relieved. 'Maybe I've now just become too suspicious of everyone's motives!'

'Suspicious? How could *anyone* ever be suspicious of me?' Dario rocked back on his heels with mock-injured innocence. 'I have no secrets. Everything I do is completely transparent. With me, what you see is what you get.' The corner of his mouth twitched wryly, belying his words.

'I'm not so sure about that,' said Josie, remembering the way he had clammed up on her that first day, when she'd suggested there might be skeletons in his past.

'Then take my word for it. Work aside, are you enjoying your stay here?' he said as they strolled along.

'I'm loving every minute,' Josie said. Walking along beside Dario, through a beautiful Italian castle, she was living her most exotic fantasy. 'It's all wonderful—far beyond anything I've experienced before.' She shook her head in wonder until the diamond drops of her borrowed earrings tinkled.

Dario looked down at her, his eyes dark and thoughtful. He knew he could take her, that tonight she was his. Yet suddenly he found himself wanting more from her than just her body. He wanted her to know more of him, to show her something of himself—something more intimate even than the kisses they'd shared. Impulsively, he said, 'Let me show you what I've been working on today.'

Lifting her plate and glass from her hands, he put them on the nearest wide stone window-sill. Then he gravely offered her his arm. With a thrill of daring, Josie put her hand into the crook of his elbow. With a smile of triumph, he led her out through the quadrangle, beneath the boughs of the ancient apricot tree towards the privacy of his artist's studio.

# CHAPTER NINE

'Wow! So this is what you get up to!' Josie breathed as Dario opened the door to a small modern office unit, discreetly sited away from the *castello*.

Dario had real artistic skill. She could see that before she crossed the threshold of the building. His work was everywhere. Bright abstracts and stylized still-life studies hung from the walls, stood on easels or leaned against shelves neatly lined with equipment. His eye for composition was obvious, he had a free and easy way with media of all types and a real feeling for colour.

'You'll never see it all from there.'

He put his arm lightly around her shoulder to draw her inside. At first Josie was distracted by the warmth of his touch, but then her curiosity got the better of her. She moved away to inspect a Rothko-inspired piece waiting to be finished off.

'You could do this professionally, Dario.'

'Yes, but I'm not going to. You, on the other hand, really could do something with your talent.'

'And the equipment you sent me. In all the excitement, I forgot to thank you for it.' Turning to him, she rose on tiptoe and spontaneously kissed him on the cheek. 'Thank you, Dario.'

'You're very welcome,' he said warmly. This evening was turning out to be a revelation on so many levels. Not even Tamara or other women like her, in his bed or out of it, could make him feel so alive. Josie had attracted him from the first moment he'd seen her. Those reckless moments in the clearing had been wonderful while they'd lasted, but coming out with Arietta's name had wrecked everything. He had been working through an emotional hangover since then, unable to expose himself again. And then Josie had appeared at his party. Not only that, but she had made it very clear that she was here to enjoy everything he had to offer. *Everything.*

His chest tightened and his breathing became shallow. His heart was pounding, but this time it was more measured than at the picnic. When he looked at Josie tonight, he felt no trace of betraying his past. Arietta would never leave him, but he wouldn't allow her memory to intrude this time. Tonight, he felt transformed. A weight he hadn't realised he had been carrying fell away from his shoulders. It freed him to enjoy Josie's company, and anything else that she might suggest.

'It's a beautiful evening,' he said, his voice husky with anticipation. 'We don't want to waste it stuck in here. Why don't we take advantage of it?'

*And each other,* he thought as they stepped out into the warm, dark night. She looked so lovely he was almost afraid to touch her, for fear she might break.

He took her hand and squeezed it. In response,

she moved in close to him. The evening was so peaceful, he could hear his own pulse and knew Arietta was slipping away from him with every heartbeat. He could not forget her completely—but she would never again cast such a long shadow over his life. With a pang of guilt mixed with relief, he realised that was a good thing. It was something else he could celebrate with Josie tonight.

She was gazing up at the night sky. He escorted her away from his studio, taking care to make his movements casual and unforced so as not to alarm her and break the spell.

The evening was alive as they strolled across the *castello*'s inner courtyard. Crickets chirruped and the breeze brought the fragrance of wild honeysuckle whispering in from beyond the high walls surrounding them. Then the sounds of an orchestra filtered through the warm evening air.

'You have a band?'

'Not personally.' Dario smiled. 'They're hired for the evening. Listen—I love this tune, don't you?'

Before Josie knew it, she was in his arms.

Words weren't needed. The feel of his hand spreading protectively over the small of her back and his fingers lacing into hers was enough. Rocking gently, he danced her slowly around the courtyard. Taut with nerves, Josie followed his lead.

'Relax.'

He dropped his head so that it nestled against her shoulder. She could feel his breath moving in delicate ripples over her bare skin. The feel of it and the softness of his hair brushing her cheek was enough to release a shudder of longing from her body.

'I knew you'd like this song.'

'It's…incredible.'

'You deserve nothing less, Josie,' he murmured.

'I don't know about that.'

'Stop it—you always do yourself down! You've already achieved so much in your life, climbed so high, and all on your own. Tonight, you should enjoy being the most beautiful star of them all.'

Josie giggled nervously. He leaned back a little so he could search her expression.

'Why laugh? There's nothing funny about that.'

'You're right. I shouldn't have done it. It's just that…it's been a very long time since anyone said anything like that to me.'

'Then "anyone" has been most remiss.'

'There hasn't been an "anyone". Not since Andy left me,' she murmured, adding silently to herself, *and I won't want anyone else now I've had your arms around me, Dario.*

She couldn't say that out loud. It would sound too lonely and needy.

'It sounds like your Andy was a bastard.'

Josie shook her head ruefully. 'No. He was just a man with ambition. We met on the same course at university and found we had the same aims and the same dreams. At first we shared everything with each other, and planned for the future. I blamed him so much for cheating on me, but maybe…maybe we never loved each other properly. Not like—' *Not like how I'm starting to feel about you,* she almost said, before snapping her mouth closed to block the words. This giddy feeling wasn't love! It was probably just sheer relief that she was forgiving Andy, and happiness at the beauty of the night.

'You're a loyal woman not to bad-mouth him in public.'

'Oh, don't talk to me about loyalty.' She groaned. 'My mother still cooks Sunday lunch for two every weekend, just in case my father walks back through the door. I tell her that's hardly likely after ten years, but she brings a whole new meaning to the word "faithful".'

Dario's arm tightened around her. 'So your father walked out, and your fiancé abandoned you…?' His voice sounded light, but underneath he was seething with anger at the two men who had dared to treat Josie so callously. 'It's a wonder you trust any men at all.'

'I don't—which is why I'm not harbouring any illusions about *you*, Dario!'

She forced a laugh. In response, he drew her so closely in to the shelter of his body she felt a chuckle emanate from deep within him. It felt so wonderful the last remnants of her self-control began shredding away beneath the gentle movements of their dance. She stopped still, knowing she had to stop now if she was ever going to, and pulled away from his embrace, but as slowly as possible. She couldn't bear to lose contact with him until the very last moment. Knowing she was about to lose control, she made a last effort to resist.

'Thank you for a truly magical evening, Dario.'

'The pleasure was all mine.' He trailed his hands down her bare arms, reluctant to finally let her go until the last moment. Gazing at her through the dusky light, he suddenly noticed something and tutted. 'I'm afraid our dance didn't do your corsage much good.'

Josie looked down. The fleshy white sepals of

her flowers had been crushed against his broad chest. They were bruised and brown. Hoping they weren't a sign that he would leave her heart just as crushed, Josie sighed. 'That's such a shame. I was going to get them preserved as a souvenir of this wonderful evening. They won't keep now.'

Dario's hand moved again, but this time to take her arm. 'Then you'll need a replacement. There are plenty of flowers out in the rose garden.'

He drew her gently in the direction of a door set into the high stone wall surrounding the courtyard. Opening it, the first thing she experienced was a wave of birdsong, rising up from the distance. Then the overwhelming perfume of a thousand roses swept her away.

At her gasp, he smiled. 'Nightingale Valley is living up to its name tonight.'

'My goodness,' she breathed. Dario looked at her, admiring the purity of her profile in the moonlight, her eyes alight with joy. The flowers forgotten, he linked his hands around her waist and drew her near again.

'I have a confession to make, Josie.'

She looked up at him questioningly.

'The fact is, I had a very selfish reason for holding this party. And, as a man who has become used to having anything he wants, I couldn't deny myself.'

She looked up. He was smiling.

'So? What was the reason?' *Surely not just to seduce me!* she thought breathlessly.

'You'll think it's really stupid.'

She clapped her hands flat to his chest. 'Try me.'

He gave a humourless laugh. 'Remember what I said about birthdays, and how Antonia and I were always forgotten? Well, when I inherited the *castello* I swore to make every birthday really special. I'm beyond the age when I make the date public, but that doesn't mean I have to deny myself a party. And today's the day.'

Josie was enchanted. 'Oh, Dario! Happy birthday! But why didn't you or Toni tell me? I would have got you a present and a card—instead, I've got nothing...'

Somewhere, in the back of her mind, the penny dropped. It had been tossed across that designer's salon by Antonia and now bounced around inside her brain, but Josie was far more concerned with the look on Dario's face.

He grimaced again. 'That's another reason why I don't broadcast the date. As you've said yourself, anything I want, I already have. Why should I put my friends to the trouble and expense of buying me things?'

Josie was shocked and couldn't help showing it. 'Birthdays have got nothing to do with money. That's not what presents are about!'

He stared at her, genuinely intrigued. 'Isn't it?'

'No!' Josie pulled away from him emphatically. 'They're a way of reminding people that their friends care enough about them to give them something in honour of the day.'

He gave her a look, as though he was waiting for further explanation.

'I would have taken the time to choose something you really wanted. Something for your studio, maybe. I'm sure there are all sorts of little things you need—new colours, brushes... the sort of thing that it would be too much of a bother for you to break off and go out and buy for yourself.'

'That's what the Internet is for—and why I employ staff.'

Josie sighed with annoyance. 'It's the gesture that matters, not the thing itself.'

His mouth moved, but then he must have thought better of saying anything and stayed silent. She thought of all the gestures they had shared, the looks, the touches and those kisses...

'Sometimes the greatest gifts cost nothing at all,' she added thoughtfully.

Dario waved his hand, as if brushing away the subject. 'We're not here to talk about me. Come and experience the di Sirena night, Josie.'

Taking her by the hand, he led her into the fragrance-drenched air of Nightingale Valley. One deep breath filled her full of enchantment.

'Dario…it's wonderful…' she whispered.

He chuckled. 'I thought you'd done a grand tour of the estate and would know all about this place.'

'Yes, but that was during the day, while I was working. It has taken you to open my eyes to its natural wonders. *All* of them,' she said, a thoughtful look on her face.

'It's a pleasure—and I would love to give you more,' he said, drawing her gently towards his body again. Unable to wait a moment longer, he lowered his head and kissed her full on the lips. It was a long, lingering explosion of sensations that sapped her last ounce of resistance. When their lips finally parted she leaned against him, suddenly as weak as water and trying to catch her breath.

'Did you know that kisses get lonely?' Dario's

voice was as soft as the touch of his lips against hers as he kissed her again.

It was exquisite, a perfect melding of sensations that coursed through Josie's veins like warm chocolate. A shocking, daring idea had been forming in her mind. Dario had lit the fuse and now it exploded into her brain. All the same, she had to steel herself before the words would come out.

'I know exactly what I'd like to give you for your birthday, Dario. It's something you don't have—and something no money in the world could buy.' She swallowed hard before whispering, 'Can you guess what it is?'

His dark eyes glittering in the moonlight, he looked down at her and shook his head.

'It's me,' she whispered.

He continued looking down at her, almost expressionless. Only a muscle flickering in his cheek showed the control he was exerting over his reactions. Before she knew what was happening, he was leading her across to the far side of the rose garden. There, a wooden gate opened out into the estate proper. Before letting her through it, he stopped and turned to her.

'Are you sure this is really what you want, Josie?' he asked seriously.

She smiled and nodded, not wanting to interrupt the wonderful flow of birdsong rising from the valley below them. Dario suddenly smiled at her, the tension seeming to leave his body. With one hand, he loosened his tie and undid the top button of his shirt. In the half-light, the contrast of the black velvet against the bright white of his shirt was dazzling. Taking her by the hand again, he led her down a wide woodland track, following the contours of the hillside.

'There's a lake at the bottom with a gazebo overlooking the water. You'll like it there.'

Josie knew she would like it anywhere if Dario was with her.

'I'm so glad I came to your party after all,' she whispered.

Dario paused and looked back at her. All the

shades of evening couldn't disguise the flash of his beautiful white teeth.

'I couldn't agree more.'

When they reached the lake, the gentle susurration of insects was punctuated by the plop of something small diving into the water.

'A frog,' he reassured her as she drew closer. Taking her gently in his arms, Dario's kiss was long, slow and sweet.

'You made such a spectacular entrance this evening,' he breathed at last.

'But I didn't do anything.'

'You didn't have to. A woman so poised, and looking like an angel…you took my breath away.' Always uncomfortable with praise, Josie shook her head and blushed.

'No—don't deny it. Be proud! Every woman and every man in the place couldn't take their eyes off you. You were the star—my star—and I had to spirit you away before anyone else could.'

In the breathless hush that followed his words, a nightingale burst into song from a hazel thicket within a few feet of where they stood. Josie smiled and, as Dario's touch tingled around the outline of her face to lift it for another kiss, a second bird joined in.

'Rivals for the same prize,' she whispered.

Dario's kisses made thinking about anything but him impossible. The insistent presence of his body completely enthralled her. The firm ridge of his arousal pushed against her as he held her close, cradling her in his arms. The tip of his tongue sensitised the entire curve of her neck. Josie shivered in wild anticipation and instantly he pulled off his jacket and enveloped her in it.

'I'm not cold.'

'I want to make sure you don't get that way.'

Curving an arm lightly around her shoulders, he led her towards a clearing in the trees. The full moon was just rising above the southeastern horizon, its silvery light sending rippling reflections across the lake that slept peacefully in its cool shadows. Flag irises and sweet rush stood sentinel around a palatial summer-house, complete with its own little jetty. Josie looked nervously at a small rowing boat and oars that were tied to it.

'I know you'll be happier on dry land.' Dario's low laughter lit up her face as he opened the gazebo. The small house was the perfect place for romance. Its cedar-wood walls retained the day's warmth, while beeswax polish and swags of lavender hanging from the rafters perfumed the air with the memories of summers long past.

'I want you.' Dario's voice was husky with testosterone.

When he kissed her now it was with more urgency. A slow burning fire had been kindled from the moment their eyes had first met. Now it burst into flames of unquenchable passion. When his hands began to move over her, Josie could do nothing to stop him. As he reached the voluptuous curves of her body, she gasped, throwing back her head in anticipation. Dario was quick to act, kissing the cool pale column of her throat from the tip of her chin to the hollow at its base. As his hands cupped her breasts she remembered the way his sensitive fingers had enclosed that ripe peach on the day of their picnic. A little moan of anticipation left her lips, encouraging Dario to dip his head and move his lips over the thin silk of her dress. It was so delicate, the small nubs of her erect nipples were clearly visible. They were too much of a temptation for Dario. He tried his teeth against one, gently testing its sensitivity. The effect of his teasing sent Josie into paroxysms of desire. Her fingers drove into his midnight-dark hair, pulling his head closer. Moonlight glittered over its tousled luxuriance, and Josie couldn't help herself. Sliding her hands over his shoulders, she cupped his face and brought it up level with her own.

'Take me,' she moaned in a voice barely recognisable as her own.

Dario engulfed her in his arms, plundering kiss after kiss from her willing mouth. Josie shrugged off his jacket and let her hands work their way beneath the cool white fabric of his shirt to find the red-hot elemental man inside. Soon they were both naked in the moonlight. Dario filled her senses so completely, she was barely aware of her surroundings as he laid her on the soft down-filled cushions of the summer-house sofa. His outline was sleek and hard as he towered over her, ready, willing and more than able to claim his ultimate prize. As he swooped down to cover her body, she twined her legs around his narrow waist, desperate to bring him closer to the core of her being. As he glided over her in the darkness, her body was torn with a cry of need that echoed into the night.

Long, long afterwards, Josie lay gazing out along the length of the lake. She had no idea of the time, but it must be so late it was now early. The summer night had never darkened completely. A single bright star was left in the sky. It stood high above the water, its pinpoint of light dancing on surface ripples stirred by a light breeze. The nightingales were still singing, but they had been joined by one or two sleepy robins. Dario lay with his head nestled against her neck, quite still apart from the gentle rise and fall of his breathing. Josie should have been in heaven. Instead, her mind churned over and over what had happened during the spectacular hours they had shared. Dario had stripped away all her inhibitions, taken her to paradise and kept her there. Josie thought back, exhausted and overwhelmed by the wild passion he unleashed in her. She glowed at the memory…but now she knew she couldn't get enough of him. From this moment on, nothing life could give her had a chance of competing with the night she had just spent—unless it included Dario.

And that thought was what tortured her now. This man was a playboy—a party animal to his capable, dexterous fingertips. Josie wanted his body, but knew she couldn't bear to have it without his love and loyalty as well. But that was a greedy, impossible dream. Dario was no more capable of giving her a lifelong commitment than Andy had been. Josie had finally realised just how little her ex-fiancé now meant to her, but Dario was an entirely different prospect. She wanted him with every fibre of her being—but she would never be able to keep him. No woman could hope to do that.

When he stirred, Josie knew she had to brace herself and resist him. One more encounter, one fleeting touch, one smile and she would be heading for disaster again. When his hand began to glide sleepily over her naked thigh, she took a deep breath, slipped out of his grasp and stood up.

'Dario, I...' There were no words. 'I have to go.'

To hide her expression, she turned away from him quickly and pretended to be more interested in gathering up her scattered clothes than watching him wake.

'Where are you going? It's still early—let's

start all over again...' His drowsy words simmered with promise.

Josie looked back at him. She knew it was a mistake, but she was unable to stop herself. He looked magnificent, as ever. The early sunlight played over his golden muscles, and she felt desire tighten its grip on her body again. She had to escape while she still could. One hand pressed tight against her belly, trying to restrain her desperate need for him, she looked away.

'Last night, I had the most wonderful time of my life, Dario, but I shouldn't have let it happen.'

'Why ever not? I thought it was one of your very best ideas,' he said, smiling.

Josie began to pull on her clothes anyhow.

'What I mean is, I don't want you to think that I'm asking for more than you've already given me. I don't want to force you into anything, Dario.'

Dario's smile faded. 'What are you saying?' He sat up, looking suddenly angry.

Josie struggled with her feelings. All she

wanted to do was drop everything and lean into his powerful embrace again. The only thing stopping her was the knowledge that Dario had done this dozens of times in the past, and had cast off those other girls as easily as he had thrown off his clothes the night before. She was worth more than that, and she knew it. He'd helped her know it. She would remember his searing looks scorching straight across the party towards her for as long as she lived. The only thing that could spoil that memory would be the devastation of his abandonment.

*If I end it now I can remember all the good things, without the horror that pursued me after Andy's betrayal,* she thought. *It will be so hard to let Dario go, but he would only cheat on me eventually, and that would wreck every special thing we've had.*

'I've already given you everything, Dario.'

'You say that, but I know you have much more to offer me, *tesoro,*' he said with gruff exasperation. He reached out to her, but she sidestepped before his hand could connect with her arm. 'What do you want me to say? Did you think that I was going to offer a lifelong commitment on the basis of a single night? You must know me—or at least my reputation—better than that, Josie.'

She hurriedly pulled on her beautiful dress. 'I don't want you to say anything, Dario, especially about the future. But…well, actually I…I suppose I don't know what I mean…'

He watched her for a few seconds and she saw his expression rapidly closing down. With a chill of recognition, she saw him retreating from her and the intimacy they had shared through the warm, still hours of darkness.

'I do. I've often had to say the same thing. It's a novelty to be on the receiving end, I'll admit, but I think I can help you.' He spoke the words in a way that made Josie want to run. Dario's reputation scared her enough, without needing details.

'It goes something like this: "That was a fantastic night, so let's remember it fondly and move on." That's what you're trying to tell me, isn't it?' he announced, getting up without warning and turning his back on her.

Josie stared at him. Secretly, she had been expecting, no, *hoping*, that Dario would put up at least some token resistance in the face of her brush-off. Instead, he concentrated on rescuing his clothes, which had been scattered during their reckless night of passion. She felt her insides contract with the loss of him.

*Please don't end it here—not now, not yet!* she thought. *Let me have a little more pleasure—an hour, a day, a week...*

It was no good. She knew only too well what would happen if she went down that route. One more kiss from Dario was sure to lead straight to heartbreak. Now she had tasted everything he had to give, she was too greedy to trust herself with him ever again.

*Because when my heart and mind is full of*

*him, that's when I'll discover he's 'entertaining' someone else and betraying me like Andy did.*

'You're right, Dario,' she said unsteadily. 'It was wonderful...but that's it. We'll put this down to experience. I'll be gone soon, so it would be silly to try and make anything more out of it,' she said in an offhand way, puncturing their awkward silence as she tried to get a better response from him.

'Good. You're being very sensible, as usual. It's what I've come to expect from you, Josie.' He gave that lovely hint of the exotic to her name again, and it made her cry inside.

'You shouldn't get mixed up in casual flings. You aren't the type,' he went on, strolling over to lift a skein of her hair over her shoulder. It was a gesture that was more patronising than romantic. 'But I must thank you again for your most wonderful birthday present. It was a miraculous treat—like nothing I have ever been given before.'

He rapped out his words in an oddly emotionless way and didn't look at her as he moved away again. Josie was totally deflated. They might as well have shared an evening's carp fishing.

Snapping on his watch, he checked its display. 'I'm afraid I must go—I've promised to take Antonia into town this morning. She wants my help in selecting a nursery for Fabio.'

His voice was still gritty with testosterone. That thought added a terrible twist to Josie's almost unbearable longing. She had wielded such power over his body during the hours of darkness. Then, she could have made him stay by her side with a single touch. She was desperately tempted to try again now, but it was too great a risk. His face was unreadable, but the bright searching light of day would leave her no hiding place if he rejected her. Josie was determined to learn from all the mistakes she had made in the past and not make any new ones.

When they were both dressed, Dario escorted her all the way back to the *castello*, but neither spoke.

Josie couldn't help thinking he had been silenced by regret, and that idea struck her dumb with despair.

# CHAPTER TEN

DARIO sat in his estate office later, tapping the end of a pencil against his teeth and staring at the Monet he had bought last time he was in New York. He would remember the night of his thirty-third birthday for the rest of his life, but not with pride.

He rubbed his chin thoughtfully, wincing slightly over the place where he had caught himself with the razor earlier that morning. It had been very difficult to look his reflection in the eye. Josie was affecting him in an unusual way. He always aimed to love women and leave them before either of them got hurt. He winced again. The mere thought of that four letter word 'love' made him cringe inwardly whenever he thought of Josie, and he had been thinking about her a lot over the past few hours. She was different in every way from the girls he usually dated. They weren't afraid to show their feelings. Instinctively, he had always known Josie wasn't like that. She wasn't the sort to make a fuss. She had stood up for her ex-fiancé after all, even though he had cheated on her and then walked away. Dario grimaced. He had waved goodbye to any number of women over the years, but this was his first experience of a girl waving to him first.

He checked his diary. With a lurch of concern he saw that Josie was due to leave within a week. He thought of her beautiful sunlit face that morning, and frowned. She had looked so preoccupied. What could possibly be worrying her? A surge of lust powered through his groin and he laughed at himself. Concern for a woman's state of mind hadn't troubled him for years. Wanting to experience her body again was a much more familiar urge.

For some reason he couldn't get Josie's words out of his mind.

*I'll be gone soon.*

They were true enough. Both she and Dario had known the date of her departure from the time this visit was arranged. So why had she kept mentioning it? Their exchanges in that awkwardly formal 'morning after' moment kept assaulting him in flashback.

*We'll put this down to experience.*

That agreement should have made him feel happier—after all, he had said it so many times to so many women over the years.

*Why isn't it working this time?* He ran his thumb back and forth across his lower lip. *Why not?*

He winced yet again, but not at the thought of what they had done last night. That still kept his body alight with desire. He puzzled on, gnawing at the problem like a wolf in a snare until the answer came to him in a single word.

*We.*

That word was the stumbling block. He hadn't used it since Arietta was alive—the last time he had felt part of a couple. And Josie had used it as well.

Suddenly he realised the truth—the clue to this whole problem. Josie had thought of them as a couple, not as simply a one-night stand. She didn't really want it to end yet, any more than he did. At that thought, his pulse started to race. His body tightened with an instinctive roar of possession at the very thought of her walking to another man. The strength of his reaction surprised him…terrified him.

He grasped suddenly for an image of Arietta. For a panicked moment, he couldn't recall her face. He concentrated fiercely, feeling how much he'd loved her, how he was responsible for her loss, and soon felt calmer. Josie had been right to leave. He couldn't offer her anything more than a fling, even if she wanted it. Ruthlessly ignoring the small voice which continued to protest against never holding her in his arms again, he forced his attention back to the estate.

\* \* \*

A day later, head down, Josie marched towards her camp beside the old olive press. Not even work had been able to do anything about her burning sense of shame and self-loathing since the party. *How could I have been so stupid? Dad and Andy both promised me the world, but they still walked away. If I think a rich playboy is going to be any different, then I really am fooling myself...*

Work had been such a safe haven for her until now; she had convinced herself that it was all she ever needed. Then one look at Dario and her defences had crumbled. The moment he'd taken her hand at the party, Josie had known there could be no other man for her, not even if she lived to be a hundred. But she had to face facts. Dario had a reputation as a Casanova, and no man would give that up lightly. He might have played the part of honourable Count to perfection while he'd escorted her back to the *castello*, but that would be the end of it. Josie knew only too well how easily men could change and turn away.

*Dario's lifestyle keeps admirers circling him like reef sharks. He never lingers with anyone for long, so why did I think I was any different?* she thought furiously. *I had to finish it before he got the chance to break my heart. By this time next week, he won't remember what happened between us. In a month's time, he won't even remember my name. But his effect on me will last for ever...*

There was nothing for it but to retreat into her work once more. With only a week left of her stay, the best she could do was keep her head down and try to be invisible. She desperately wanted to confide in someone, but it was impossible. Antonia was watchful and understanding but, caught between her brother and her best friend, she didn't pry and Josie couldn't bear to drag her into the situation. Instead, she spent her time working as far away from Dario's haunts as she could, but his influence ran deep. Although determined to protect her poor battered heart from any further damage, Josie couldn't stop thinking about him.

When lack of concentration caused her to chip a second piece off the stonework she was uncovering, she threw her trowel down in disgust. For as long as she was here, Dario was going to dominate her thoughts and distract her from her work. There were only two solutions to that problem, and it was decision time. She could either finish her trip early and go home right now, or she could come to terms with her feelings for Dario.

*I'm supposed to be a rational adult, so why can't I decide and stop drooping about like a love-struck schoolgirl?* she asked herself.

The answer to that was all too obvious. She wanted Dario—but she was scared. Giving him so much power over her emotions was a step too far.

*If only I could be strong enough to say goodbye...but not just yet...*

A desperate remedy swam into her overheated

brain. Perhaps she could simply let down her guard long enough to enjoy Dario for a little while longer. Just until the end of her stay at the *castello*. She could indulge herself for a few more days, but there would be a fixed time limit and they would both know it. She could experience Dario's charm and incredible lovemaking all over again, but walk away before he broke her heart. No one would have to make promises they couldn't keep. It would be nothing more than a wonderful footnote to her stay.

*Other people have holiday romances all the time and no one dies of disappointment, do they?* she reassured herself. *Why can't I, as long as I keep to the rules? If Dario can do it, then so can I. It's not as though anyone expects a fling to last. That's all I'll have to remember.*

Having convinced herself, Josie shut out her remaining doubts and packed up her tools. Then she set off to find Dario before she changed her mind.

\* \* \*

Dario was in his studio, studying the painting he had been working on. His charcoal sketches hadn't caught the right mood at all. As an act of desperation, he had tried to commit directly to canvas, hoping to be inspired all over again. But this portrait refused to work well, even after his third attempt. Sighing, he turned away to pick up a turpentine-soaked rag, ready for another try. Then a figure in the doorway caught his eye. He stopped in mid-movement. It was Josie. For a moment, he felt his expression transformed by guilt but managed to turn it into a smile.

'Come in! This is an unexpected pleasure. I was beginning to think you were avoiding me.'

Josie blushed and hesitated, and he guessed that was exactly what she had been doing. But then he saw her stiffen her resolve—obviously and beautifully. She lifted her head and straightened her shoulders. Then she stepped into the studio, but looking around more warily than she had done on their glorious evening together. He knew that must be because this was his territory—his special place, with its atmosphere thick with the perfume of media in all their forms: linseed oil, paint and new canvas. It was a place he felt safe, but Josie clearly didn't.

'Why don't you come over here and see what I'm working on?'

She walked over to him, but without the self-confident stride she used to approach her own work. When she saw the image he was about to erase, there was a definite hesitation. Although she tried to hide it, he saw her shoulders droop and her mouth turn down. Even half-finished, his work in progress was clearly a beautiful dark-haired young woman.

'Is this Arietta?' Her voice hardly disturbed the atmosphere between them.

*She must know the answer to that question already,* Dario thought. Her gaze was so direct, it made him uncomfortable. He set his jaw and hardened his expression.

'It was supposed to be her, yes.' He antici-pated her question. 'I thought she deserved her place in the di Sirena portrait gallery. After all, if things had worked out differently, she would have been my *Contessa*.'

Josie neither moved nor spoke, so Dario fixed her with a penetrating stare.

'Aren't you going to ask me about her?'

'You'll tell me if you want to,' she said quietly. 'I don't like talking about my own past. I can hardly expect you to be any different.'

He tipped his head in brief acknowledgement. 'We met when I was in my final year at university...' He couldn't find the words to frame what had happened. How they'd fallen in love almost from the first moment. It had been magical, perfect, unlike anything he'd ever known, until real life began to intrude. Looking back, he wondered how they'd have coped after university, when their idealism would have had to have changed to meet the practicalities of the world. 'We had a row one evening. Of all the stupid things, it was because I was spending too much time painting and not enough with her.

She drove off into a storm. I went after her, but she was determined to get away from me. We were both travelling much too fast. She skidded into a flooded ditch.'

He waited for the usual spasm of pain to pass through his body. It always did when he thought about that terrible evening. Always—until today. He frowned, puzzled. Josie said nothing.

*On top of everything else, she's a good listener!* he thought, and tried saying more.

'She died on the way to hospital.'

'I'm so sorry, Dario.'

'Yes.'

She looked surprised at his automatic response, and Dario realised such a quick reply might have sounded heartless.

*She's probably expecting me to sound more traumatised. I used to...but not now...*

The revelation came to him easily, but he guessed it would be difficult to live with. He wondered if saying more could distance him from his past still further.

'It nearly destroyed me,' he began hesitantly, but there was no need. Telling Josie seemed so right, it felt good to unburden himself rather hold on to the pain. 'For years, no day passed without my thoughts turning to her. After all, meeting Arietta was a defining moment in my life. After she died, I tried to fill the void she left with partying. It has never worked. Nothing could compare with the simple enjoyment of spending time with a woman who understood me, for better or worse.'

A smile flickered across his face and was gone. 'But her memory has started to slip away from me. Little by little, day by day I have begun to feel I'm losing her. At first, inheriting the *castello* and its estate kept me so busy I didn't have time for memories. Now, when I try to recapture them, she is always retreating from me.'

He stopped. Josie watched him, unblinking. She was only a heartbeat away, and he could tell she was holding her breath. He knew, because he was doing exactly the same thing.

'I've fought it every inch of the way, Josie. I started to paint a portrait of Arietta as I remembered her, but it's not going well. I've worked and worked on this damned painting, but it's impossible. I can't catch her.'

He looked at the canvas for a second, then passed a hand quickly over his face to hide the fact that he no longer cared.

Josie couldn't help herself. She rushed forward and threw her arms around him.

'Dario, don't… I'm sure Arietta would hate to think you were unhappy…'

He dropped his hand abruptly. To her relief, she saw his eyes were dry, but their depths were full of a turbulence she had never seen before.

'How can you possibly know that?'

She let him go and backed away. That reassurance had been forced out of her in a moment of pure panic.

'I…I'm sorry. I have no idea. How can I? But I'm absolutely certain that she couldn't bear to think of you being upset and living a half life, full of regret.'

'That's exactly what Arietta said to me once, all those years ago.'

He was very still for a moment, and then reached for his wallet. Opening it, he pulled out a small well-worn photograph, which he showed to Josie. Then he held it next to his half-finished painting.

'Do you see the likeness?' he asked grimly.

Josie looked from the painting to the photo-graph, then back again.

'Well...' She hesitated, not wanting to say what she really thought.

'My painting doesn't look much like the girl in the photograph, does it?'

'You did say you were working from memory.'

'Yes. Exactly.'

Dario was staring at the picture with an un-fathomable expression. Josie joined him. The photograph of Arietta was in black and white, but his painting was in glorious colour. Josie

voice trailed away. Living each day without Dario had been agony for her, yet he seemed so unmoved! If he didn't accept what she was about to say, the pain would be unspeakable, yet she knew she had to seize the moment and at least try, otherwise she'd never forgive herself for being a coward. 'There's no reason why we can't be...*friends* for the rest of my stay. Is there?' she added hurriedly.

Dario went absolutely still for a moment, then turned to clear up his brushes and paints. When he replied, his words were slow and considered.

'Josie, of course I want that. But let's be absolutely clear—I don't want any more misunderstandings. There must be no chance of anyone getting hurt by mistake.'

Josie didn't reply at once, but eventually, she stammered, 'W...we're both adults, aren't we?'

'All right, then. However, you'll have to take the lead. I don't want you to end up regretting anything.' The words seemed gentle, yet the tension around his jaw gave the impression of a lethal predator, barely held in check.

Josie couldn't speak, so she simply nodded. Dario turned away from the building tension, and began to scrub his canvas clean. She watched him, strangely relieved that Arietta's image would soon be erased.

'What are you going to paint now?'

He stopped to fold the cloth he held into a pad.

'I haven't decided yet,' he responded finally.

'Then…how about me?' Her voice was quiet, but clear.

Dario turned slowly towards her and smiled. It was like the sun coming out from behind a cloud that had lingered for far too long.

'Seriously?'

She hesitated for a moment, then nodded.

'Then yes—I'd love to do that. And…I think I'd like to paint you wearing the stunning dress you wore at the party. The green silk wrapping that covered my wonderful present,' he said softly.

Looking out over the beautiful view from his studio window, Josie pretended to think. She couldn't. Her mind was filled with images of a much more seductive kind than mere landscape.

'The zip of that dress is rather tricky…it's not something I could manage on my own. I might need your help to get it on and off,' she whispered, leaving no doubt about who was taking the lead now.

Outside, the last swallows slipped through the sky with the sound of roughened fingertips on silk. Then Dario took the few steps that still separated them and slid his arms around Josie's waist. She closed her eyes.

'So why not give in and let me help you for once?' he whispered into the citrus-scented softness of her hair.

The touch of his breath on her neck sent shivers over her skin. Lust flooded through her body with an urgency that wouldn't wait for bed. When his hands guided her into turning and facing him, she couldn't resist. Their first kiss was a slow, haunting moment of quiet bliss. Then Josie opened her eyes and found herself looking over his shoulder—straight at the unfinished portrait of Arietta. Her blood ran cold.

'You feel chilly,' Dario murmured, running his hands over her bare arms with lingering appreciation.

'A breeze must have blown in from the garden. You'd better close the blinds,' she whispered. He smiled and did so, then turned to her, his eyes asking a question. Josie gathered her courage for a final time and let herself speak the absolute truth. 'I want you, Dario. Now.'

He looked down at her, the smile lingering on his lips, but his dark eyes were hooded and intense. 'This is the last chance you have to change your mind.'

'I want you right now. It doesn't matter where we are,' she said huskily.

'That's exactly what I was thinking, *tesoro.*'

He pulled away from her, slowly and reluctantly. Still greedy for contact with her, his hand slid down from her shoulder to her hand and finally kissed each of her fingertips in turn before letting go of her. Then Josie took control as she had promised, her heightened state of arousal urging her on. Undressing Dario was a triumph of restraint over animal need. She forced herself to take her time, kissing every inch of skin she exposed. His hands roamed over her, wild and free. She could hear the hiss of his breath and knew he was struggling against his most basic urge to take command. Knowing that acted as a powerful aphrodisiac. Sliding his clothes off over the hard, hot planes of his body and hearing the swish of fine designer fabrics brushing against his skin was so exciting it lured Josie into trying things she had never been tempted to do before.

'All my experience counts for nothing,' he breathed into the still, warm air.

'You don't know what it means to hear you say that, Dario.' The thought of being able to please him made her actions feel all the more erotic. When he took hold of her now, she did nothing to stop him. She was bathed in a state of such

high arousal, she wanted to be taken and pos-
sessed and to hell with the consequences.

'You are divine…' His words were as seductive as the urgent pressure of his body against
hers. '*Dio*, but you are everything I have ever
wanted in a woman. I want you so much…'

She wanted him, too, with a passion more deep
and urgent than anything she had ever known
before. With a wordless sound of anticipation,
he lifted her onto a low velvet-covered couch in
the centre of the room. There, he took possession
of her. They made love with a fast, fiery intensity that neither had experienced before—and
Josie knew that from now on she would never
find happiness with anyone but Dario. When
he couldn't hold back any more, she enfolded
him, holding him so close that she felt they were
both part of one body. In response, he shouted
his pleasure to the skies in one glorious burst of
fulfilment.

# CHAPTER ELEVEN

OVER the next few glorious days, Josie completely lost track of time. She was in Dario's arms, and it was the only thing that mattered to her in any way. She was completely absorbed by him, and her feelings were reflected and magnified in his fascination for her. The two of them became one in a delicious spell of seduction, but Josie was also acutely aware that there was a time limit on her happiness. She had to get back to the project that had first brought her into the charmed embrace of Dario's influence, before her time in Italy was over.

Catching her hand as she got out of bed one morning, he turned it over and kissed his way from the delicate skin on the inside of her wrist to the bend of her elbow. She gasped, barely resisting the temptation of Dario's husky 'Come back to bed?'

She forced herself to draw a line between the two parts of her life, pleasure and work.

He let her go, but when she bent to kiss him goodbye he almost persuaded her to stay. Returning her passion, he kissed her with such fire it drew all the breath from her body.

'No…stop, I must go, Dario!' she gasped, laughing—but her heart wanted her to stay for ever.

Watching Josie leave his room filled Dario with a cocktail of feelings. His body wanted her more than ever, but his mind had lost all sense of direction. Josie was so different from the other women who had populated his life so far. They always began to lose their appeal the moment he had satisfied his lust. That hadn't happened with Josie. Instead of becoming easier to resist over time, he was beginning to find it hard to decide where he stopped and she began. They had been inseparable since that moment she'd walked back into his studio. Their five-hour fling had now stretched into days, and Dario no longer had any idea of how it would end.

Gazing out of his bedroom window over his sunlit estate, he saw Federico's flock of doves circling over the courtyard. Josie must have thrown them some croissant crumbs as she left. As he smiled at the image, one downy feather detached itself from the flock and swung through the air. Caught by a little up-draught, it suddenly spiralled towards the blue sky again.

*Funny,* he thought as he decided to get up and follow Josie out to her work. *This whole business started because I wanted to keep her at arm's length. Now we might as well be riding on that feather, hovering between heaven and earth.*

It was a journey Josie assumed would be over by the following weekend. She already sighed softly each time Dario opened his appointments diary. His smile widened. Josie had given him the perfect birthday present, but he'd been planning for a few days and now he knew that she would be getting an even bigger surprise—from him!

Work was a constant thread running through Josie's life. She could never forsake it entirely, especially as she knew it would be the only thing left to comfort her when Dario was a painful memory, haunting her every moment.

*Dario...*

She softened at the mere thought of his name. She was almost powerless to resist him. She spent seductive nights wrapped in his arms, and was awakened by his kisses and passion each morning. He was encouraging her to take a more relaxed attitude to life. His influence over her was growing so much that she'd even dropped her famous independence long enough to let him take her visiting his friends. Dario had a formidable network of contacts. He introduced her to people whose private estates contained spectacular ruins, many of which had never been excavated before. Some were interested in hosting parts of Josie's intended field trips, so she arranged follow-up visits to survey the sites. This was where Dario sprang his biggest surprise of all. Instead of sitting on shady terraces sipping cocktails with his contacts, he was only interested in working at her side.

On days like today he was always there for her, but Josie was sure it wouldn't last. When her visit to the Castello Sirena ended she would leave, like the swallows. Dario couldn't follow her. Instead, he would forget her the moment autumn chills chased all thoughts of their shared summer days away…

The day before she was due to leave for England, Josie was out on site when her phone rang. Dario had been delayed back at the *castello* by paperwork, so she was waiting expectantly for his call. She answered on the first ring.

*With luck, he's going to say he's on his way,* she thought.

'Josie!'

It wasn't the voice she so wanted to hear, and her spirits sank.

'Bursar,' she replied evenly, managing to hide her disappointment. 'I didn't realise you knew my mobile number. I'm afraid I'm in Italy at the moment, so selling any more raffle tickets for university funds is out of the question,' she added, hoping he wouldn't ask her why until she'd had time to dream up some excuse.

'I know where you are, dear girl. That's why I'm ringing you. I have some good news.'

Josie racked her brain. She knew how this man worked. Money was everything to him: if he called her 'dear girl' she must have more of it than he did.

*The chance would be a fine thing,* she thought. *Unless—*

'Don't tell me the staff's syndicate numbers came up in the lottery last night?'

'Ah...no, but in a way you're on the right track.

Remind me—how much money did you request to fund your research and field trips, dear girl?'

His cheery tone convinced Josie that he was building up to ask her some tremendous favour.

'That depends.'

'Well…why don't you think of a number and double it, say, to allow for inflation…wear and tear, that sort of thing?'

There was definitely something up, and there was only one way to flush this particular pigeon out of the undergrowth. Josie picked an enormous figure out of the air. 'Sixty thousand pounds.'

'Is that all?' The bursar sounded disappointed. 'Couldn't you make it a round hundred? Taking into account travelling costs, expenses, et cetera, et cetera?'

'Oh, *easily*,' Josie said with heavy sarcasm. 'It was the government's loss when I decided not to become a Member of Parliament.'

The bursar laughed like a drain.

*He* never *laughs at my jokes*, Josie thought.

*The sun must really be shining out of me today.*
Consumed with curiosity, she tried pushing
the envelope a bit further to see if it came back
stuffed with used notes.

'Why stop there? Why not make it two hundred thousand, to allow for shrinkage?'

'Oh, now, don't let's be greedy!' The bursar chuckled. 'Count Dario is being generous
enough in letting you name your own price.'

Josie froze. 'What?'

'Count Dario di Sirena is so impressed with
the work you've been doing on his estate, he
wants to fund your plans to develop student field
trips to the area. He thinks it will boost the local
economy, so he's willing to finance your stay in
Italy for as long as is necessary, and pay for all
your research, too.'

Josie stiffened. 'Oh, he *is*, is he?'

'Yes. We've had some good long chats on the
telephone. What a *very* nice chap he is!'

'Delightful.'

'He told me how much he enjoys seeing you

working about the old place and bringing it to life. He's really interested in being of service to you, Josie.'

'Hmm.'

'Yes, he seemed extremely concerned that any financial constraints put on you by the university shouldn't curtail your ambitions.'

'Concerned? I'll bet he was. Hang on, Bursar. I need to discuss this matter with the Count myself, before we decide *anything*,' she announced, grimly determined that the only nice round figure she would accept from Dario would be a big fat zero.

Dario was sitting in his office, contemplating the di Sirena Monet that hung opposite his desk, when his peace was shattered by a whirlwind in human form. Josie was glowing from her half-mile hike across country and burning with righteous indignation.

'What the *hell* do you think you're doing?'

Dario could see from the way she slammed the

door that 'Thinking of you' was obviously not the answer she wanted. He smiled instead, and gave her a chance to explain. It was a mistake.

'How dare you extend my stay without asking me? And how dare you pay off my department? I've had to grovel for every penny I've ever needed, yet I start sleeping with you and suddenly money is flowing in my direction faster than your flattery! How do you think that makes me feel, Dario?' she hissed.

Startled by her reaction but determined not to show it, he netted his fingers and watched her over them. 'Not grateful, that's for sure,' he drawled.

Her face changed. 'I won't be forced to rely on anyone else's...' she seemed about to say something else but then plumped for '...money. You're trying to make me dependent on you.'

'I thought you understood me better than that, Josie,' he replied in a more reasonable tone of voice. 'I think I understand *you* quite well. You're brilliant at your job and deserve to go as far as possible, yet I've heard you speak about how you have to beg for a share of the limited amount available, and you never get enough to use as you'd like on your projects. I have more money than I can possibly spend so, to me, the answer was obvious.'

Josie plonked her hands down on the edge of his table and leaned over to glare straight into his face. 'Maybe it is, to you. In fact you're just another hypocrite! And God knows what you've made me look like in front of my colleagues!'

Dario stood up sharply, making her jump back. 'What have they got to do with anything that goes on here? And as for calling me a hypocrite—*dannazione*! This funding for your project would mean you could stay here for longer. You don't want to leave here tomorrow any more than I want you to go—so what's hypocritical about trying to keep you here? I'm trying to help, Josie. Whatever is wrong with that?' Dario continued, exasperated. 'What *is* wrong with you?'

'Nothing!' she yelled—although he noticed she could no longer meet his gaze. 'Unless you call honesty and integrity faults!'

'It's a bit difficult holding a conversation with you when you're so far up on your high horse!' he retorted. 'Why don't you come down to earth so we can discuss this like adults?'

'Oh, would you *listen* to yourself?'

'No—you listen to *me*!' he snapped back. 'At first I thought you were too delicate a flower to get involved with me. Now you come bursting in here like poison ivy! If you really want the truth, I wanted to make up for the way you've been treated in the past. What's so bad about that?'

'Just about everything! Can't you see?'

'No!' Dario flopped back in his chair, throwing up his hands in disbelief. 'How can you say that?'

'*I* want to be in charge of what I feel and what I do and where I go, and by paying money to try and keep me here, you've made me feel like a…like a common…' Josie couldn't bring herself to say the word, but it was obvious which one she had in mind.

Dario's jaw dropped when he realised what she meant. 'How dare you? I would never dream of paying a woman to sleep with me,' he said coldly.

'You don't have to! You've got power, prestige, influence, social standing—what woman wouldn't want a part of that?' she yelled.

'Not you, obviously.'

She stared at him, hot and red and breathing very fast.

Making a supreme effort, Dario wrenched his attention back from her pulsating breasts to her face. It was funny how every tiny detail had fixed itself so firmly in his mind—the slight gap between her teeth, the way she kept brushing her hair behind her ears when she was angry—*or nervous*, he found himself thinking.

'This is it, Dario,' she said in a voice full of venom. 'I don't want to be your mistress any more.'

That was a shock. 'Really? I don't remember asking you to become my mistress in the first place. I didn't think that was the arrangement.'

Her angry flush became the nervous pink of embarrassment.

'S...stop it! You didn't have to ask me. N...not in so many words. You wanted my body and... and...and, I wanted yours...' She blushed even deeper at the admission. 'I was only going to be here for a little while. That's why we agreed to enjoy this while it lasted, and then put it all down to experience.'

'But we're both getting so much enjoyment, so much *pleasure* out of your stay. Why don't you like the idea of extending it?'

*Because I can't stop wanting you!*

'This isn't about the length of my stay, Dario! Can't you see what you've done? I've lobbied and argued and written and rung everyone I could think of for months and months, trying to get funding for my project, but nobody's taken me seriously. Then you push a pile of cash at them and *ecco*! *E*verything's fine and dandy. But you can't see how this makes me feel—and, what's worse, you'll *never* understand—not in a million years!'

She burst into noisy tears of rage and frustration.

Dario stared at her. His sister was the only person he had seen cry real tears before. It was such a shocking sight, it took him a few seconds to react. Then in a flash of movement he was on his feet and pulling Josie into his arms. That made her howl all the louder. His arms full of weeping woman, Dario wondered how and why they were getting further and further away from the gentle dwindling of passion and eventual amicable parting he'd had in mind.

He heard her snivel something that might have been 'I'm a total failure…' and held her closer still.

'How can you say that?' he asked in a reply that could cover all sorts of eventualities. It seemed to work. There was an unsteady pause in her tears.

'I've always known it,' she said slowly, her words still stippled with tears, 'because every time I let anybody get under my skin, it all goes wrong. First my dad walked out, then my fiancé, and now you're trying to lead me into the same trap! Not even work can save me this time. I was happy here while there was a strict time limit. I could accept that, and it meant I didn't have to worry about our future. I knew we didn't have one. Now you've extended my stay here.'

'But that's a good thing! Isn't it?'

With a final sniff, she put her hands on his chest and levered herself back to look up at him. It was time to be honest.

'No, it isn't.' She closed her eyes and sighed heavily. 'You just don't get it, do you? This was supposed to be nothing more than a fling. I only allowed myself to sleep with you because I'd convinced myself that I could handle it on that basis. Now you've changed the rules, how is that supposed to make me feel? Guess!'

'Quite frankly, I can't.'

She gritted her teeth. 'It's setting me up for disaster. You'll find someone else, exactly like Andy did. The only difference is, this time I'll be expecting it. It'll be like sitting on a ticking time bomb. When it goes off and you leave me, I'll be convinced, once and for all, that I'm emotionally hopeless and ought to avoid any contact with other people ever again!'

'What?' He was incredulous. 'How can you say that? It's not true—and you can't simply shut yourself away! Everybody loves you!'

'No, they don't. *You* don't, for a start. And you never will.' Her eyes blazed, and he could see she was struggling very hard to control herself.

'But…think of all the goodwill there is for you, back in England,' he said, manfully hiding his desperation. This had started life as such a brilliant idea, but here was Josie, scattering his plans to the four winds. Dario was amazed to find that his usual caution had deserted him. Josie was hurting and he wanted to make her feel better, but he had no idea how. His own feelings had to be forgotten while he tried to salvage the situation.

'If they thought anything of me or my work at all, they would have given me enough money to do what I wanted in the first place. You wouldn't have had to go behind my back like this.'

'Josie! Try looking at this rationally. There's only one reason why they didn't give you all the money you needed—because it wasn't there to be given,' Dario said firmly. 'That's why the university was so delighted to accept my offer. All the people I spoke to there were full of praise for you. They would have loved to support you more, if only they'd been able to. In fact, before I stepped in they were worried that some other institution would head-hunt you.'

Hiccuping back her tears, Josie looked up at him suspiciously.

'You're making it up.'

He looked back at her with the smallest suspicion of a smile. 'Would a faithless playboy lie to you about something serious like that?'

'He might, if he thought it would get him back into my good books.'

'I think too much of you to lie, Josie.'

They both went very still—and then Dario frowned.

'…I mean as a friend of the family, of course. I didn't mean to upset you. All I wanted to do was to give you a nice surprise. It was nothing more than that.'

To his utter horror, Josie burst into floods of tears again.

'Whatever is the matter now?' Dario asked before a sudden flash of insight hit him. 'What's *really* upsetting you?'

'Don't you know?'

He shook his head, which only made her misery worse. He felt her pull in a huge shuddering breath before confronting him one last time.

'Thanks to you, I have to go back to England

right now anyway because I love you and you couldn't care less about me and if I stay you'll dump me and it'll break my heart all over again and I won't be able to bear it!' she wailed in one long drawn-out howl of agony, before dragging herself from his sheltering arms and running straight out of the room.

Dario was so stunned he let her go. He had obviously read the situation all wrong, but he didn't have a clue how to put things right. He suppressed a desperate impulse to go chasing after her because he had no idea what to do or say. The awful suspicion that he would only make a terrible situation worse kept him trapped inside his office.

He thought about his portrait of Josie, wearing her lovely green dress. It was still incomplete because work on it had been interrupted so often by their desire for each other.

*And now it will never be finished,* he thought with a pang of realisation as the true scale of this disaster suddenly came home to him. *I've lost her just as surely as I lost Arietta.*

The name pierced him like an arrow, but in a way he didn't expect. It wasn't with the pain of sorrow, but with the shock of revelation.

For Arietta would *never* have spoken to him as Josie had done.

Storming back to her own rooms, Josie dressed, piled everything into her suitcases and scrawled a note asking for all her equipment to be packed up and sent back to England. The last thing she did was take her beautiful green cocktail dress from its padded hanger. She gazed at it for a long time before laying it down on a sheet of tissue paper and folding it reverently for its trip to England. Yet striking all her colleagues dumb at the university Christmas ball was the very last thing on her mind now.

All she wanted to do was get as far away from Dario as possible.

* * *

*No, Arietta wouldn't have spoken to me like that,* Dario thought with growing unease. *She would never have put up with me keeping a light alive for another woman in the first place.*

He remembered how he had fought with Arietta on the night she'd died. If he had let her come back in her own time, and not provoked her into going too fast as she went into that bend, his life would have turned out very differently.

*And I wouldn't be standing here, resisting the temptation to go after Josie and tell her a few home truths,* he thought bitterly. Knowing he was in the same building as she was, but separated from her by a huge gulf of misunderstanding, was unbearable. Abandoning his work, he strode out to his studio and turned her unfinished portrait to face the wall. Then he began methodically going through his tubes and pans of paint, and rinsing brushes. The only alternatives were to risk her dashing off for ever, or force a showdown that could have no winners.

Dario was the tenth Count di Sirena.

Aristocrats didn't do that sort of thing. His ancestors had ruled by the sword and they were afraid of nothing. Josie knew that. He thought of her now in her new manifestation as a bouncing fireball of defiance and suddenly, strangely, he wanted to laugh.

*She's brave, I'll give her that,* he thought. *What a Contessa she would have made!*

That really did make him smile. It was an expression he couldn't sustain, because loving was something Dario had convinced himself he could live without. Letting another woman into his life would mean reliving all the agony he had suffered over Arietta, and he couldn't do it. *If I give in now then somehow, some day, I'd lose Josie too, and I couldn't bear to go through all that pain a second time.*

'As though living like *this* is any better!' he yelled, suddenly grabbing the nearest thing to hand and sending it flying across his studio.

It was a box of willow charcoal. It hit the wall and burst, sending brittle black shards in all directions. The sooty explosion brought Dario to his senses. Shocked, he went to retrieve what he could. As he did so, he passed the window and caught sight of the landscape he knew so well. It made him stop and think. For hundreds of years his forebears had fought and died for these glorious acres. If they had been afraid of what *might* happen, the di Sirena family would have died out long ago and Dario wouldn't now be enjoying the heady mix of joy and responsibility that made up his life. Those warriors had lived their lives to the full, and to hell with tomorrow.

Josie had been as brave as any of his sword-wielding ancestors and, in refusing to risk his heart a second time, Dario knew he had lost her.

Antonia was upset to see Josie leave, but she was too good a friend to pry. Everything was arranged with Castello Sirena efficiency, from a car to take Josie out to the *castello*'s airstrip, to her premature flight back to England. By the time everything was organised, the arid anger and despair that had forced Josie to storm away from Dario had faded. Now regret lodged in her throat like a cherry stone. She had been afraid this would happen, and sure enough her nightmare had come true. Why had she been stupid enough to let herself fall under Dario's spell?

*Because I hoped history wouldn't repeat itself,* she thought bitterly. *It's the same mistake every woman makes.*

She twisted her damp handkerchief between her hands, unable to believe that the man who made her feel like the only woman in the world could still end up hurting her so grievously. To take her mind off her pain, she checked her documents. Then she did it a second time. After that, she went through her handbag, over and over again. Counting change and flicking through her diary passed a few more minutes, but not enough. When a mutter of annoyance rippled through the di Sirena staff she looked up, glad of any distraction. Through the glass wall of their office, she could see someone on the phone.

The ground crew were summoned. She watched them straggling into the room. They were some distance away, but the office door had been left open. Josie tried to hear enough without looking as though she was listening. She could only make out a few words, but that was all it took to throw her into a panic.

Dario was coming.

He must have given orders to delay her flight on the di Sirena jet. Josie had never felt so angry—or so alone.

At the worst possible moment, her phone announced an incoming text. With a distracted cry she grabbed it, then stopped and stared.

It was from Dario. The two short, simple words he'd sent her made no sense, but they still had the same effect as a blow to her head. Totally absorbed by his message, she stood up, but why, she didn't know. Then everything and everybody else in the aircraft hangar suddenly faded away from her consciousness. A little bubble of silence grew to envelop her. She glanced around wildly. Then she looked back at the display on her phone, as if by some miracle the characters had morphed into something more understandable. They still made no sense. Two words—after all the thousands of words she had wasted on Dario... It must be a mistake. It *had* to be. What else was she supposed to think? That he could be as cruel as he was unthinking?

A terrible rumbling sound echoed through the whole airstrip building. It was like thunder, but Josie knew thunder wouldn't reverberate up through her feet like that. And a storm would stop outside the main doors...

This one didn't. It was Dario. He was riding Ferrari, galloping the horse so fast he couldn't stop. They hurtled straight into the hangar before he managed to pull up in a plunging, wheeling rattle of hooves.

'Well, Josie? What is your answer?'

She stared at him. He was pale, breathless and as focused on her as ever.

'No.'

He flung himself off his horse. Slapping it on the rump, he sent it back to the stables while he cornered Josie.

'No? What do you mean, *no*?'

'Exactly what I say. What are you trying to do to me, Dario? You mess up my life and then suddenly, out of the blue, you send me a text as though the past few hours had never happened. What do you think I am? A masochist, or simply insane?'

'Marry me.'

It had been a shock to read it as a message on her phone. Now it was more than that.

Josie looked at him and saw the truth. This was the last gamble of a desperate man. His expression was hunted, and his normally tidy hair windblown. She noticed a strange base note to the usually subtle fragrance of his aftershave. Later she realised it must be the tang of adrenalin, but at that moment all she could concentrate on was how she was going to get through the next few minutes. She breathed unevenly, trying to steady her nerves, but she found things had gone too far for that.

'That didn't make any sense when you sent it as a text, Dario. Saying it out loud doesn't make it any more sensible.'

'It's what you want. *It must be what you want,*' he repeated, his voice rising.

From somewhere in the distance came the faint sound of the ground crew. They had an audience. For the first time in her life, Josie didn't care what anyone else saw, heard or thought. All she was interested in was Dario. She gazed at him, not knowing whether to laugh or cry.

'You sound like a man who is trying hard to convince himself.'

'I am convinced—because deep in my heart I know you want me, and I want you—'

Josie covered her face with her hands. 'No… you want my body, that's all. And yes, I want yours, too. But marriage is a partnership for life, Dario. I don't think you understand what that means,' she sighed.

'You're wrong—*wrong*, Josie! I know *exactly* how marriage works!' he growled through gritted teeth. 'I spent years watching my parents tearing each other apart. You think I've refused to commit before now simply because of Arietta? You don't know the half of it. There were times when I would have paid a king's ransom to get away from the unhappy life sentence that was my parents' marriage. They couldn't divorce: my father didn't want to be the first in his family line to break rank. My mother was too fond of his money and the position in society it gave her.'

Josie was shocked. 'Then why in the world do you think that proposing marriage to me will be the answer to all your problems?'

'I don't.'

It was a clumsy, hurtful answer. Realising that, Dario swore under his breath and tried again.

'It's because I know nothing less than marriage will keep you here at my side.'

Josie looked at him narrowly. 'Go on.'

'What do you mean?'

'There must be more to it than that. You've told me your parents put you off marriage. Proposing to me must seem like running your head into a matrimonial noose! You don't need an heir, you've got Fabio, so it can't be because you've suddenly decided you require a legitimate son. Women flock around you. There must be something else.'

His eyes locked with hers. They were dark as jet as he said, 'I once told a woman I loved her, and she left me.'

'Arietta didn't leave you, she died.'

It was cruel, but Josie had long since stopped feeling kind when it came to Dario's relationships with other women.

'Yes.' He gazed at her with naked anguish. 'And I killed her. For years I've been telling myself I sent her car into that ditch as surely as if I had been driving it myself. I chased her away, Josie.'

'But it didn't stop you racing after me,' she said slowly.

She saw the colour drain away from his golden skin. He nodded.

'It was a risk I had to take. I couldn't bear the thought of you boarding that plane and flying out of my life. It wiped every other thought clean from my mind.'

He slumped down in the seat beside hers. Once again she saw him rub at his face as though trying to erase all his bad memories. Knowing what he must be going through but feeling powerless to help, Josie waited.

'When you first walked into my life, it brought back memories of how happy I had been—and how devastated I was when Arietta died,' he said eventually. 'I couldn't bear to lay myself open to that torture again. That's why, when Fabio was born, I made him my heir. I couldn't imagine letting any woman so far into my life that there could ever be the possibility of children. Until a few weeks ago it simply wasn't an option. Like you, I had learned that it was less painful to keep everyone at arm's length. That was why, when you stormed out on me this morning, I pretended I could leave you to come to your senses. I thought it was your loss, and that I didn't care. But it wasn't true. An awful fear began to crawl over me that one day I would forget you, the way I've forgotten Arietta. I don't want to do that, Josie. Not ever.'

It was too much. In the face of his confession, Josie's own injured feelings meant nothing. Forgetting all her resolutions, good and bad, she reached out and gently slipped her arms around him as he sat beside her. When he didn't resist, she leaned against him and laid her head against his chest.

'Does this mean you understand?'

'Maybe.' She nodded, and then felt him swallow hard.

Josie closed her eyes. Tears were very close, and she didn't want to weaken.

'I love you, Dario—more than you could ever imagine…but it won't work. I can't hope to compete for your love on the same level with Arietta.

Don't you see? I've got all sorts of human failings, but she's an angel—*your* angel.'

'That's got nothing to do with the way I feel about you, Josie,' he said quietly. 'The pain of losing Arietta will never go away, but I don't feel the same about it now. My father was right when he asked me at the time what I knew about love. My answer then was "everything", but in truth it was less than nothing. *At the time*.'

'You weren't likely to learn much about love from him, by the sound of it,' Josie muttered, half to herself. She felt Dario's hand run over her back until it came to rest lightly on her shoulder.

'And it's why I think you should reconsider your proposal very carefully, Dario,' she continued with a sudden return of common sense. 'You've told me that the pain of losing Arietta stopped you risking your heart again, but falling in love is never going to be easy. Sometimes you just have to take a chance. I've been here before, so it's a scary place for me, too. I need to know I'll be getting all of you, not just tantalising glimpses of the loving, caring man you really are, deep down inside. How can you promise me this is for ever and not just until you get scared and back off?'

It was a long time before Dario could answer. 'A di Sirena is never scared.'

Josie lifted her chin and met his glittering black gaze with defiance. 'Then prove it to me.'

'No. I don't need to.' His voice rose dangerously, attracting the attention of everyone in the building. 'I've already done everything I can to prove how much I need you. There's only one thing left to say: Josie Street, I love you. I want you, body, heart, soul and spirit for as long as I live. Nothing else matters,' he said in a crescendo of passion that left her speechless and wide-eyed with wonder.

Their audience of ground crew erupted in noisy excitement, but Josie hardly noticed. She was at the still, small centre of a universe that consisted only of Dario. He was looking down at her with such intensity that nothing else mattered to her. Josie knew she wanted him more than any other man in the world, and always would. It was madness to hesitate even for a second, but she wanted to be too sensible to be bounced into a quick answer.

Suddenly it was all too much. The arguments, the worry, all the uncertainty… Her eyes filled with tears. That only added anger to her maelstrom of emotions. This was what she had wanted all along, wasn't it? For Dario to put her first and show that he loved her? Well, statements didn't come much more explicit than a public proposal of marriage.

'Dario, I'm scared…' she began, then saw he looked as stricken as she was. She wanted him with all her heart, but didn't know if she was brave enough to accept the challenge.

'This is all wrong! You told me you don't do meaningful relationships, and now I know why. You might think you want me now, but it won't last,' she said slowly, reliving the darkest days of her last betrayal.

'Do you think I care about other women, now I've met you?'

At the harsh sound of his words her thoughts fled and all she could do was gaze at him. The suave, sophisticated man who had charmed her from the instant they'd met had vanished. Dario was streaked with sweat from his desperate ride across country. He wouldn't have done that for any of the fragile beauties who had drifted around the *castello* at his last party—but he had done it for her.

'I...I don't know,' she said cautiously.

'No—and neither did I until the moment you tried to run out of my life, Josie. When Arietta died, it ripped all the heart from me. For years I managed to live without it. I simply existed, passing time. You changed all that. For the first time since losing Arietta, I started to enjoy the world around me. I began to anticipate the future, instead of merely looking forward to the next party. Isn't that enough? What we've found in each other is really good.'

'I know!' she burst out, unable to keep silent.

He pressed his lips together, trying to hold back the ultimate confession. 'I've given you far more of myself over these past few weeks than I've offered any other woman,' he admitted in a low voice. 'A little of me was more than enough for them.'

'Yes, but it isn't enough for me!' she blazed. 'I'm worth more than all of your other women put together!'

Horrified at her own outburst, she slapped her hands over her mouth, but it was too late. Stricken, she gazed at him.

He gave a silent whistle. 'That's quite an admission, coming from you. Shy, self-effacing Dr Josie Street.'

'I know. I'm sorry,' she said in a small voice.

'I didn't mean it as criticism. It was a compliment.'

Josie blinked. The effect was like rubbing sandpaper over her eyes. That could be the only reason her eyes started watering again.

'You were right about me, too, Josie. I've spent too long wallpapering over the cracks in my life. It took you to show me there's more to life than shallow pleasures. Without you, I'm nothing but an empty shell. I love you. Marry me. Will you?'

'Oh, Dario,' she breathed. 'Don't you know the answer?'

'I will never get used to this,' Josie murmured a few days later, as they watched workmen clambering over scaffolding set up along the lime avenue. The boughs of each tree were being spangled with fairy lights, ready for the grand party Dario had arranged to announce their engagement. Guests visiting the *castello* would have the best of both worlds. During the day, their arrival would be serenaded by bees and golden orioles. When they left, their way would be lit by a million coloured stars.

'Oh, I'm sure you will.' Dario's arm circled her waist and he drew her close to kiss her hair. It was flowing loose around her shoulders today, exactly as he liked it. He enjoyed its clean, sweet fragrance for a while, then added, 'But just in case you need a little help, I've arranged something special for you. Your mother is coming over for our party this weekend.'

Josie looked up at him, her eyes alight.

'Dario, that's fantastic—but how did you manage that? I tried so hard to convince her, but she's always been too nervous to travel abroad before!'

He squeezed her playfully. 'I've arranged everything for her, from passport to transport, door to door. All she has to do is pack.'

'You really have thought of everything,' Josie said in wonder. 'And you did all this...for me?' It was impossible to keep a note of disbelief out of her voice.

'Of course. If it makes you happy, *cara*, then nothing is impossible. I would move the stars in the sky for you,' he said softly, and then kissed her until all her thoughts flew away.

\* \* \* \* \*